HAWK

HAWK

JENNIFER DANCE

DUNDURN
TORONTO

Project editor: Allison Hirst
Editor: Allister Thompson
Design: Jennifer Gallinger
Cover design: Laura Boyle
Printer: Webcom

Library and Archives Canada Cataloguing in Publication

Dance, Jennifer, author
    Hawk / Jennifer Dance.

Issued in print and electronic formats.
ISBN 978-1-4597-3184-4 (paperback).--ISBN 978-1-4597-3185-1 (pdf).--
ISBN 978-1-4597-3186-8 (epub)

    I. Title.

PS8607.A548H39 2016   jC813'.6   C2015-907905-5
                                               C2015-907906-3

2   3   4   5   6   21   20   19   18   17

Conseil des Arts du Canada   Canada Council for the Arts

Canadä

ONTARIO ARTS COUNCIL
CONSEIL DES ARTS DE L'ONTARIO
an Ontario government agency
un organisme du gouvernement de l'Ontario

We acknowledge the support of the Canada Council for the Arts and the Ontario Arts Council for our publishing program. We also acknowledge the financial support of the Government of Canada through the Canada Book Fund and Livres Canada Books, and the Government of Ontario through the Ontario Book Publishing Tax Credit and the Ontario Media Development Corporation.

Care has been taken to trace the ownership of copyright material used in this book. The author and the publisher welcome any information enabling them to rectify any references or credits in subsequent editions.

— J. Kirk Howard, President

The publisher is not responsible for websites or their content unless they are owned by the publisher.

Printed and bound in Canada.

VISIT US AT
Dundurn.com | @dundurnpress | Facebook.com/dundurnpress | Pinterest.com/dundurnpress

Dundurn
3 Church Street, Suite 500
Toronto, Ontario, Canada
M5E 1M2

MIX
Paper from
responsible sources
FSC® C004071

Dear Reader

Hawk is a story about the Alberta Oil Sands. It shows the conflict within a family whose livelihood depends on the oil sands industry but whose health is also affected by it. I travelled to Northern Alberta to research this story, hoping to find a balance between opposing views of the industry, seeing first-hand the scale of the environmental and human impact.

My hope is that Hawk will raise awareness and promote thought and discussion among young Canadians, motivating them to help safeguard our people, our animals, our land, and our water.

— Jennifer Dance

*To Joanna, James, Erin, Kate, Tarik,
Matthew, and Kim — for simply being!*

"Men and nature must work hand in hand. The throwing out of balance of the resources of nature throws out of balance also the lives of men."

— Franklin D. Roosevelt, 1935

CHAPTER ONE

Fort McMurray, Alberta, Canada

Less than an hour ago, I was Adam, the long-distance runner. Now I'm Adam, the boy who ...

I can't even bring myself to say it.

The car engine dies, and I realize that we are in the garage, yet I have no recollection of the drive home from Dr. Miller's office.

I stare through the windshield. The walls of the garage swim around me. My thoughts won't move past *this can't be happening*.

Angela walks around the car and opens my door. She's my mother, but I never call her that. I figure she hasn't earned the title. She didn't raise me. Neither did my father. Most of the time, I don't call *him* anything, but when I have to use a name, I call him Frank. I enjoy rubbing both their noses in the fact that although they *are* my biological parents, that's as far as it goes. They never were and never will be Mom and Dad. They left me up in Fort Chipewyan when I was a baby, and they didn't reclaim me until I was eight! Like I was a piece of lost luggage.

"It will be okay," Angela says. "It will be okay."

I climb out of the car and follow her into the house like a zombie. She's like a zombie too, stuck on a repeat cycle of *it will be okay*.

I kick off my shoes and leave them where they lie. Angela puts them on the mat alongside hers. A question hits me like an arrow in the heart: how much longer will Angela have to deal with my mess? How much longer will she have to deal with *me*?

I feel strange, like I'm floating, not walking. Angela hands me the mail, and I put it on the kitchen counter. It's the same routine as before, but *nothing* is the same as before. Everything is different. An hour ago, I would have pounced on the McDonald's flyer, stuffing the coupons in my pocket, but now I couldn't care less.

Life as I know it is over.

CHAPTER TWO

The female fish hawk is returning from the heavy humidity of the Texas marshes to the cool, crisp air of Northern Alberta where she was born, to the place where memory tells her that lakes and rivers are filled with fish, and men are few and far between. She has never made the migration in this direction, yet she knows the way.

She is here to find a mate.

With a roar, the plane races down the runway. The wheels leave the ground, and we rise into the air, the nose pointing steeply toward the bright blue sky. My stomach gets left behind, but that's normal for me these days. I often feel as if I'm in several different pieces, all of them trying to stay together.

In seconds, Fort McMurray becomes a toy town, with Highway 63 stretched out like a piece of knotted string. I recognize the downtown core and then the miniature houses of Thickwood where I live. It should be exciting. It's not. I'm numb.

Briefly, before the plane turns, I see the oil sands to the north, a strange, dull emptiness merging with the distant horizon. No forest. Nothing green. Just hazy brown sky and a landscape the colour of mud. In some strange way I feel as if I'm looking at myself … used up, depleted, empty.

The plane levels out, and we start our journey south. I look down on the river meandering in S-shaped loops through spruce-green wilderness. I know that I'm flying in the opposite direction of the flow. *It's* going north, up to Lake Athabasca, where I grew up. A distant memory comes to me: water lapping gently against sand, and a little boat tipped upside down under the trees. For a second my heart feels like it might burst out of my chest. I can't believe that I miss the old place. It's been over six years since I left there and came south to live with Frank and Angela in Fort McMurray. I knew that McMurray was the oil-boom town, so I'd thought it would be dirty and oily and smoky. But it's not! The sky is usually bright blue, and trees are everywhere. In summer, it's like living in a green bowl with a river flowing right through the middle. In winter … not so much.

When I first arrived, I thought the coolest thing was the fast food. You could get anything — burgers, fries, pizza. Definitely better than eating fish all the time. Whether it was baked, stewed, fried, or made into soup, it was all still fish. The next best thing was the TV. My grandfather had an ancient box with rabbit ears that was right out of prehistoric times, so Frank's flat-screen with countless channels kept me spellbound for hours. Even so, it wasn't good enough for him. He soon replaced it with a thinner one, and now we have an awesome seventy-inch model. It's almost like going to the movies.

At the beginning, Frank and Angela showered me with clothes and toys and video games. They were trying to buy me, but I didn't care. I took it as payback for the years they gave me nothing. And I never gave an inch of affection in return. They still give me things, but the toys have morphed into the latest iPhone, iPad, and Wii, and the clothes include the best running gear on the market. So why is the old place on the shore of Lake Athabasca tugging at my heart? It doesn't even have a McDonald's. It doesn't make sense. McMurray is my home. There's fun stuff to do here, and people to do it with, and more girls to see in a minute than I would see all year up in Chip. My stomach lurches. I'm flying toward a very different future, one that I'm sure doesn't involve fun, fast food, or girls. My heart sinks even lower at the thought of Chrissie, the only girl I've thought about for months, or did before all *this* hijacked my life. What are my chances with her now? Zip.

For the briefest moment, I see a bird flying north. I wish I was going with it. Instead I'm heading south, to Edmonton, to the Stollery Children's Hospital. And I'm scared.

There's nothing I can do.

I'm powerless.

I wipe my clammy palms on my jeans and force myself to breathe deeply, the way my running coach has taught me. It doesn't help.

Angela is in the seat next to me, her fingers working the rosary beads in her lap. She's praying under her breath. But when I listen hard, I hear the same phrase that she's been mumbling all week. "It will be okay. It will be okay."

I don't believe her. I don't think that she believes herself, either.

We fly through cloud. It hangs against the window, thick and damp and grey. I can't see outside, any more than I can see my own future. I'm flying blind. It's daunting.

There's a jolt as the plane touches down. We've landed, yet I have little recollection of the last part of the flight. I've been reliving the day just two weeks ago when a grim-faced doctor pronounced two words that changed my life.

"It's leukemia."

Angela gasped.

I knew vaguely what leukemia was, but in hope that I was mistaken, I blurted out, "What's leukemia?"

"Cancer of the white blood cells —"

My pulse pounded in my ears, drowning out the doctor's words. I felt strange, as if I was outside myself looking in. Occasional words pierced the fog: three-and-a-half years' treatment ... Edmonton ... Calgary ... Children's hospital ... Ronald McDonald...

"Do you have any questions, Adam?" the doctor asked.

I wanted to know what Ronald McDonald had to do with anything. I didn't ask. My voice had vanished.

Angela unclips her seat belt, the metallic clunk bringing me abruptly back to my surroundings. I get out of my seat and follow her up the aisle of the plane to the exit, moving oddly, almost gliding, feeling as if the contents of my head are floating along a few inches behind. Angela looks back at me. She's tired, I can tell. Her eyes are red and puffy. Briefly, I catch a look of pity on her face, and then it's gone, replaced with a determined but silent *it will be okay.*

Life has changed. And although part of me hopes that I'm in a nightmare and will wake up soon, somewhere deep inside I know that things will *never* be the same.

CHAPTER THREE

From high in a clear blue sky, the fish hawk scans the land for one particular fish-bearing river. She sees its familiar shape and knows she is nearly home. She now searches for the tall, dry spruce where her parents had raised her, high above the reach of predators. Her powerful eyes spot a squirrel scampering up a tree and a mouse darting across open ground. Her cousin, the red-tailed hawk, would have pounced on these meals, but the fish hawk is not interested in small land creatures. She eats only fish.

She continues searching, but something isn't right.

If you're going to fight a terminal illness, I guess this is the best place to do it. It's bright and cheerful-looking here at Stollery. Everyone is really nice, and the doctors and nurses seem to know what they're doing.

But I don't want to be here in the oncology ward.

I don't want to see kids with bald heads and skinny arms and gown-covered, stick-like bodies.

I don't want to look like them. I don't want to be stripped of everything I am. I was second in last year's cross-country meet for all the schools in the Wood Buffalo Region. I plan to win gold this year.

I mean I *planned* to win gold this year.

How the hell can this be happening to me?

I'm hundreds of kilometres from home, and I don't know what lies ahead. I don't know what they're going to do to me, how much it will hurt, or how much pain I can take. My future is one huge question mark, and although I hate to admit it, I'm scared, really scared. Even though Angela is here with me, I feel completely alone. I can't talk to her. She left me when I was a baby, and I don't think I'll *ever* forgive her for that. Or Frank. Several times since they reclaimed me, Angela has told me how hard it was for her leaving me in Fort Chipewyan with my grandfather.

Hello! How about asking how hard it was for me!

Both she and Frank told me they did it for *me*, because they wanted me to have all of the opportunities that they never had. They said they had to leave Fort Chip to be trained and get good jobs, *blah-blah-blah*. I didn't buy it then, and I still don't buy it now. They left me! It was my grandfather who took care of me all those years. Recently, Frank and Angela have changed their story. They tell me they were just kids themselves when I was born, so they needed to grow up before they could raise me. They say I'm old enough now to understand. But they are wrong, because I still don't understand. They are always wrong — about everything.

Eventually, once they figured out they'd "grown up enough," they sent me a one-way plane ticket. They told me my grandfather was coming to live with us too. "Soon," they had said. But *soon* turned out to be more than six years. He moved to McMurray just a couple of months ago, and I'm pretty sure that my parents only flew him down here because they'd heard rumours about school kids doing drugs and getting arrested, committing suicide, or getting pregnant. Frank and Angela must have figured my grandfather could provide round-the-clock daycare while they were both working. Like I need a babysitter — come on, I'm almost fifteen!

All the same, I was looking forward to him coming. I thought it was going to be great, because I remember being happy when I lived with him. But when he arrived, everything was different. With the four of us under one roof, everyone was on edge.

Before my grandfather came, Frank would tell me to be respectful to my elders, and by that he meant *him*. But I never saw *him* doing anything that earned my respect, so I never gave it. And now that my grandfather lives with us, Frank isn't respectful to *him* at all. In fact, the two of them can't get along. Frank is such a hypocrite. He only gets along with Angela. And I don't get along with either of them. My grandfather is the only one I feel any affection for, but he's so stuck in the old ways that it's like he's from another planet, and we have nothing in common. When everyone is in the house at the same time, I stay in my bedroom. My grandfather does the same. It's a good thing that both Frank and Angela work shifts, or we'd never come down to eat!

Now that I'm stuck here in the hospital, the idea of living in a house where four people are at war sounds half decent. If I could go home, I'd be nicer to them — if only I didn't have to be *here*.

Here! There are ten beds in this ward, and the other nine kids all look much worse than me. Some of them are totally bald. I can't even tell for sure if they're guys or girls! And their age is anyone's guess. When I first got here, most of them stared at me silently. A few said "hi." I didn't say it back. Angela smiled at them, whispering to me that I should be nice and make friends. But I didn't want to be nice. And I still don't. I don't want to make friends. Not here. Because all the kids here have cancer with a capital C. How can I be one of them? I tell myself I'm going to wake up soon, and this will all have been a bad dream. But it's no dream. I'm awake. There are ten beds, and I'm in one of them.

One in ten: it's a statistic that has been plaguing me since I left Dr. Miller's office when Angela told me over and over that everything would be okay. She said the survival rate for leukemia is much better than it used to be, and that I have a 90 percent chance of becoming cancer-free and living a completely normal life. She said it quite a few times. Perhaps she was trying to convince *herself* that it was true.

When I think about getting 90 percent on a test, it seems really high. But instead of focusing on *that*, I focus on the 10 percent of people who fail the test; the 10 percent of people who will *die*. To me, that sounds really high too. *One in ten.* Five days ago, I didn't think *I* would be the one. Three days ago I considered that I *might* be the one. But today, in this ward with exactly ten beds, the possibility is crushing me, and my insides heave. *One in ten.* My chest tightens, and my skin prickles. *One of these ten.* My heart does a powerful thump, and my body feels as if I've been zapped with electricity. Then anger comes out of nowhere. I want to hit someone … or something. But the last few days have shown me that even punching pillows turns my knuckles blue with bruises.

I want to escape. I want to run, like I did in the old days, mile after mile, leaping streams and fallen logs, past the colourful flags flapping in the breeze and the cheering crowd near the finish line. But even then, I want to keep running, my feet falling on the trail until there's no trail left.

Run? I almost laugh, it's so ridiculous. I'm worn out just from climbing into bed! The only thing that can still run is my imagination.

And I'm totally scared of where that might take me.

CHAPTER FOUR

The air is filled with pockets of turbulence that ruffle the hawk's feathers, pitching her from side to side. She angles her tail and flaps hard to stay on course. This blustery wind is generally a sign of bad weather. Past experience tells her to take cover in the forest before the wind and rain knock her from the sky, but looking down, she realizes that the boreal forest is no longer there. Overhead, the sun droops toward the western horizon, assuring her she is still on course, but beneath her wings, nothing is recognizable.

Everything has changed.

Angela goes away to do some paperwork. She promises to be back soon. Left to my own depressing thoughts, I contemplate life without running. I bury my head in the pillow, hold my breath, and will myself to die. Nothing happens.

I toss the pillow aside and come up gasping for air. I pull the covers over my head and try to pretend that I'm somewhere else. It works for a few seconds, but I can't escape my dark thoughts for long. They turn suddenly toward Gemma and how mad I am at her. How could she just disappear like she did? I thought she was my best friend. People who don't know us think we're brother and sister, which is nuts because she's Italian Canadian! But I see what they mean. She looks more First Nations than I do! She tans really quickly in summer, so her skin is as dark as mine, and she has straight black hair. But hers is long, and she wears it in a pony-tail. Plus we both love running and we both want to win. She's definitely the fastest girl at Mercredi High, and I'm the top guy, but even so, we push each other to do better because we both want to win at the Regionals. We train together and hang out afterward, going for burgers or our favourite, New York Fries, even though our coach says we shouldn't eat that crap. We're inseparable. We *were* inseparable. As soon as she heard I had cancer … she vanished. What kind of best friend does that? It really sucks! I want to vent about everything I'm going through, and she's not here! I'm *mad* at her. It's not fair: *she* can still run. I can't. Maybe that's what bugs me the most.

I breathe deeply and repeat the phrase that I always recite before a race: *Be still. Be present. Breathe.* It doesn't work. The memory of the last time I saw Gemma gnaws at me with fresh disappointment. The week I got my diagnosis, she came by the house with a get-well card from the runners at the Mac Island Club, but she just handed the card to Angela and left. By the time I dragged myself to the front door, she was long gone. If I'd had the energy, I would have followed her out into the street and told her what she could do with that card. Instead, I started to text her a really mean message, but I deleted it and tried again, hammering my thumbs on the screen so hard that Angela warned me not to break my phone. In the end, I tossed the phone down and just screamed inside my head, *I hate you, Gemma!*

I tried to hide the tears that pooled in my eyes, but Angela saw them, which was the worst. I hung on to the tears, though. I didn't let them spill. At least Angela didn't say something stupid, like *Don't cry ...* or *everything will be okay.* She told me that Gemma probably didn't stick around for a visit because she didn't know what to say to me. I wouldn't know what to say to me, either. I'm not the same person Gemma liked to hang with. I can't run. I can't go out for burgers and fries. And I don't want to play video games where we just start over when we use up all of our lives. The last few days have shown me that death isn't like that. Plus now I'm miles away from home, so she couldn't visit even if she wanted to. She could phone, though, or email, or text.

Angela says I should give Gemma more time to come to terms with what's happening to me, but it's not fair! *I'm* the one who's sick. She should be giving *me* time, not the other way around.

I feel like a shaken bottle of Coke ready to explode, ready to spew rage everywhere. I clench my teeth to hold it in and repeat my mantra: *Be still. Be present. Breathe.*

Maybe it works a little. When I think about it, Gemma might have been mad at me *before* I got my diagnosis. Our relationship had changed, for sure. During the spring we spent less time running and more time walking. That was fine with me, because I was always tired — now I know why — but walking gave Gemma more time to talk. Even though she was my best friend, I often tuned out her constant chatter and let my thoughts turn to Chrissie, a girl from school who I really liked. But then, out of the blue, while we were walking along the trail, Gemma stopped and kissed me. Just like that! I have nothing against kissing, but the problem was it felt all wrong … like kissing your sister. Not at all the way I imagined kissing Chrissie would be. Anyway, I pushed Gemma away, saying something about being loyal to Chrissie, which was stupid, since Chrissie barely knew I existed then, and Gemma knew that. Anyway, she said it was fine, and she seemed okay with it. She said we needed to train harder, and she took off down the trail, running so fast I couldn't catch up with her.

I wonder now if I hurt her feelings.

Being stuck here in the hospital with nothing but my own thoughts makes me wonder about a lot of things.

CHAPTER FIVE

Beneath the fish hawk's weary wings, man-machines belch smoke and kick up swirling dust. She blinks and flies on through the haze. The scent of pine gives way to a smell that she recognizes from her southern home: the smoky stench that billows from the metal trees that grow in the warm ocean; the reek of the glossy slick that sometimes floats on the balmy water there, making it shimmer with rainbow colours. She has learned that this is not a good place to hunt. Not a good place to be.

The ward lights have been turned down low, but I can still see things dimly.

My bed is cocooned by curtains. Angela is trying to settle down on the narrow cot at my side. She doesn't have to stay here. The government will pay for a hotel room, one of the few perks of being First Nations, but she insists on staying, at least until I've settled in. Her long black hair is stark against the white pillow. She curls up and then stretches out, obviously not comfortable, but then again, neither am I. A feeling of thankfulness spreads over me like a warm blanket. I'm glad that she's here and that I'm not alone.

She's been really nice to me since I got my diagnosis. She's always been nice to me, but this is different. I wonder if she's trying to make up for the first eight years of my life when she barely knew me, or maybe the last six, when we've lived together in the same house but have been miles apart. I guess it's just possible that during those six years, the problem might have been with me. I never let her get close, even though she told me how sorry she was for leaving me with my grandfather all those years ago. She said that if she had her life to live over, she wouldn't make that same mistake. Part of me wanted to believe her — it still does. But part of me wanted to hurt her, to make her pay for abandoning me. Now I don't know what to think. It's too much for my brain to handle. I'm relieved I'm not alone, though, so I'm kind of glad that Angela is here. Yes, I'm definitely glad that she is here.

"Good night, Adam," she whispers.

"G'night," I say, the word *mom* almost coming from my lips, but not quite.

Soon she's breathing rhythmically, and I know she's sleeping. I'm desperate to sleep too, to escape from here. But the mattress is too hard and the pillow is too soft. I toss and turn. I try breathing deeply, but nothing helps because my mind won't switch off. It wanders back to Track and Field Day at Father Mercredi, just two weeks ago. I have to run the final leg of the boys' 4 x 100-metre relay, because I'm the runner. It's who I am. Or rather, it's who I *was*. But I'm *not* a sprinter, and I tell them that. I'm a *distance* runner. There's a big difference! But they don't listen. My team is in first place as I take over the baton for the last leg. The crowd is roaring, and my legs are pumping, but they refuse to fly like they normally do, and my lungs are burning. One boy passes me, and then another. I throw myself across the finish line and collapse on the grass, gasping for air. My team curses me. I'm ticked that everyone is blaming me for losing. "I'm *not* a sprinter," I repeat. "I'm a *distance* runner. I told you that. It's your own fault."

Mr. Seeton, the Phys. Ed teacher, is disappointed in me too. He says I need to work harder, that I've lost my drive. Just because he arranged for me to train for free on the indoor track at Mac Island, he thinks I owe him something. All through the winter I'd pounded that track, telling myself I was going to be the best cross-country runner, not only in Fort McMurray, but in all of Wood Buffalo Region. But as winter dragged on, running wasn't the fun that it used to be. I told myself that the indoor track was the problem. I wanted winter to end so that I could run under the sky instead of the grey metal roof that made me feel trapped.

The ice was gone from the trails by mid-April, and the mud dried quickly in the warm sun. Gemma and I started running the track that carves its way through the ravine down to the river. It didn't help. I was still tired. She would take the lead with a spring in her step, changing her stride from the sandy gravel of the main trail to the spongy moss in the depths of the forest, and then to the boardwalk over the marsh, while I'd struggle just placing one foot in front of the other.

Angela noticed how tired I was and said that I was going through changes, that I was in a growth spurt, and that tiredness is a normal part of growing up. She said that boys especially can get sore legs when they're growing fast. They even have a name for it: growing pains. She said it would pass. She was wrong. She always is.

The kid in the bed next to me is crying. He's about six years old, and his mother isn't with him. I feel sad for him. A nurse comes, drawing the curtain with a soft swish. I wonder if I will ever get any sleep here. I'm so tired but my mind won't stop spinning. It returns yet again to the track meet at school....

I get that loser feeling again of knowing that I'd let the others down. I hate it. I'd desperately wanted that day to be over so I could get out of the heat, lie on the sofa, and watch TV. Instead, I'd flopped on the grass under the trees, swigging from my water bottle and pouring the rest over my head in a futile attempt to re-energize. The announcer called for long-jump competitors to make their way to the pit. I dragged myself up, happy at least that this was the last event of the day.

When I finally got home, I staggered through the front door, throwing my gear aside. My running shoes were laced tightly to my feet. They wouldn't kick off, and I didn't have the energy to untie them, so I stumbled to the family room and collapsed face-down on the sofa.

"Adam!" Angela scolded.

I rolled my eyes at the thought that my mother was already home from work. At the same time, I realized why my grandfather was not at the door to greet me — he was up in his room, keeping out of Angela's way.

"Oh, my goodness! What happened?" she exclaimed.

I had no idea what she was talking about.

"That bruise on the back of your leg?"

I swivelled to where Angela was pointing. There was a dark bruise all over my thigh. I yanked my shorts up higher. The bruise went right on up to my backside. "What the …?"

"What happened?"

I had to think for a moment before it came back to me. "Oh, yeah, I did long-jump. I covered a good distance with my feet, but then I fell backward and sat down in the sandpit. It didn't hurt, though."

"There's no way you could have gotten a bruise that bad, that fast … unless the long-jump pit has rocks in it. Is anyone pushing you around?"

"No!"

I remember the look of concern on her face. "If someone was bullying you, or being mean to you, you'd tell me, wouldn't you?"

"Of course I'd tell you," I said, thinking that Angela would be the last person I'd tell. "I guess I landed harder than I thought."

She unlaced my running shoes, prying them from my feet. "You look exhausted. Go on up to bed. I'll bring you a snack in a few minutes."

But it was like my body had moulded itself into the sofa so that we were inseparable. Angela brought a pillow and a blanket and told me to stay there and sleep. The words were barely out of her mouth when I felt myself slipping away.

When I woke up, I was face-down on the pillow in a warm, wet puddle. I remember swiping my hand across my mouth, figuring it was drool. It was damp and sticky on the side of my face, and my hair was matted. It smelled a bit like metal. That's when I realized it was blood!

I yelled, and Angela came running. Within seconds she was dialling 911. The paramedics got the bleeding mostly under control, and by the time we arrived at the emergency department of the hospital, I felt like a fake. "It was just a nosebleed," I said sheepishly. But the doctors didn't treat me like it was just a nosebleed. They asked questions and took vials of blood. Then they parked me in a corridor on a rolling stretcher to keep me under observation for the evening. Nothing else happened, so they sent me home.

Two days later, we were back at the Northern Lights Hospital, waiting to see Dr. Miller. The receptionist didn't make eye contact when she asked for my health card. I got a bad feeling. We sat down. We waited. Angela had a magazine on her lap, but she wasn't reading it. She never turned the page, even though she stared at it for ages. I tapped my foot and drummed my fingers. But before long I was too tired to tap, or drum, and it seemed just fine to sit and do nothing.

Finally, the doctor invited us into his office. There wasn't so much as a *hello, how are you?* At least not that I remember. He just dropped the bomb.

"It's leukemia."

On the drive home, I was speechless. That was when Angela had started her one-sentence loop: "It will be okay, it will be okay." Occasionally she threw in: "We'll get through this."

I remember walking into the house. It was still the same house I'd lived in for more than six years, no different from how it was when I'd left it three hours before. But it *was* different. Everything was different. It was weird, like my body was walking around, going through the motions of behaving normally, but my brain was a few steps behind — or to be more accurate, above. I hoped that it would drop back into my body real soon, because I felt seriously out of sync.

"What did the doctor say?" my grandfather asked as soon as we got in the door.

"I've got leukemia!" I blurted out, trying the words on for size, seeing how they would sound out loud for the very first time. They sounded fine. But I couldn't look at my grandfather. I stared dumbly at my feet and then climbed the stairs to my room.

"Try to nap," Angela called out as I disappeared. "It's been a tiring morning."

She was right, but my mind wouldn't let me sleep then, any more than it will let me sleep now. It kept replaying the scene in the doctor's office. Unfortunately, it only replayed the few parts that I remembered. Gaping black holes had swallowed part of the story, leaving it like a partly finished jigsaw puzzle, or more like one that was just started. I wish I'd paid better attention. It was all so confusing. And unbelievable. It still is.

Later, I heard Angela go to her room and phone Frank. The door wasn't closed. I heard her side of the conversation.

"No, Frank, surgery won't help … No! They can't cut it out. It's not a tumour! The cancer cells float around in the blood. They don't clump together to form a tumour … No! Listen to me, Frank … There's nothing to cut out … He'll have to have chemotherapy … Radiation? I don't know. Right now they're saying chemotherapy … It's the only option. It works in 90 percent of cases … Please, Frank, stop! Don't go there."

CHAPTER SIX

The female fish hawk can still see the big river, but the thick forest that should have lined its banks and provided her with a nesting site for the summer is mostly gone. Only a narrow band of greenery remains, not enough to offer her protection and seclusion. Away from the scrawny trees, the naked earth ripples like the beaches of her winter home where the ocean ebbs and flows, tugging the grains of sand and rearranging them. But there is no ocean here to leave its imprint on the land. She loses her bearings. She doesn't know how high she is flying. She doesn't know what direction she is going. She is simply flying.

In that moment between being asleep and being awake, I think I'm at home, in my own bed, in my own room, surrounded by my own things. A marathon runner stares down at me from the wall, his bones and muscles showing as if he's been opened up. Clean clothes spill out of the closet and dirty ones are all over the floor. When I was little, Angela tidied my room, but now I don't let her set foot inside. She obeys the DO NOT ENTER sign on the door. When the mess piles up too high, or when the mood strikes me, I grab up all the trampled clothes and dump them in the laundry room. They reappear clean and neatly folded.

There's a smell I can't place. I open my eyes. I'm in the hospital! My stomach lurches. I close my eyes again, hoping not to face it all, but I can't go back to sleep. I can't stop thinking about how much has changed in so little time. Just a month or two back I was fine. Or I thought I was. I thought I just had growing pains!

I remember the last Saturday in April, the day that the ice broke on the Athabasca River. This is always a big deal for everyone who lives in Fort McMurray. It happens each spring, but it's still a shock, jolting us all back to what we were doing when the river broke the previous year, or the year before that, or in my parents' case, fourteen years before. We're in the truck, all of us: Frank, Angela, my grandfather, and me. We don't do family outings, so this is unusual. We're going to Energyse, where Frank works, because today is tree-planting day, and employees and their families have been invited to help in the final stage of a reclamation project. My grandfather says that this is a really important part of the mining process and that since the public is not normally allowed in, we should go check out what's going on. I can think of a million better ways to spend my Saturday, sleeping being Number One on the list, but I allow my grandfather to convince me we'll have a good time.

We head down Thickwood Boulevard to join Highway 63, Frank at the wheel of the new pickup truck, Angela next to him, and me in the back seat with my grandfather. Everyone's in an okay mood, at least so far, but we've only been on the road for three minutes.

We swing around the bend, and the river comes into view. Yesterday it was flat enough to drive a snowmobile on. Today it's something else, filled to overflowing with ice blocks the size of minivans. It looks like someone tipped way too many ice cubes into a container that's too small to hold them — except it's on a giant scale.

My parents, who rarely see eye-to-eye, both say, "It's early this year — it must be global warming." Then Angela gives me her annual warning about not running alongside the river, because ice blocks can explode onto the trail without warning — killing people! One day the river is frozen flat, and then the next morning it has buckled and cracked and is hurling up car-sized blocks of ice at unsuspecting runners. I don't get it.

We leave the broken river in the valley and take the highway that curves up through the forest. On the sides of the road, under the lodgepole pines and poplars, there are still a few patches of old crusted snow, almost black from the traffic and melting fast.

The sun streams through the truck window, and I close my eyes, enjoying the warmth and the bright orange glow that shines behind my eyelids. The cold, dark winter is finally done. Summer stretches ahead. Despite the exhaustion of my growth spurts and my apathy for life in general, I'm happy to be soaking up the sun.

I've lived in McMurray for so long, but this is the first time I've ever travelled *north* of town to where Frank works. It feels good, like it's the way I'm supposed to go. But that makes no sense, because there's no way I want to return to the nothingness of the North. I can't imagine life without the Sports Centre, without the climbing wall, the running tracks, the movies and the mall — without New York Fries and Boston Pizza.

"Is the traffic always this bad?" my grandfather asks, flinching away from the window as yet another transport truck thunders toward us. He still freaks out at things here — he's a newbie. In Chip you're more likely to see an ATV on the road than a car, and from what I remember, the word "crowd" means … let's say five people.

"This is the busiest highway in Alberta," Frank explains. "All the mines use it. It's the only way in and the only way out."

A transport truck roars up behind us and sits on our bumper, giving a blast on its horn that makes even Angela almost jump out of her skin. My grandfather looks horrified. Frank puts his foot down and we surge ahead.

The needle on the speedometer hits 130, and we leave the big transport truck behind. I see Frank's smile in the rear-view mirror.

Angela hangs on to Frank's arm as if her life depends on it, begging him to slow down. He gives in, and when the needle swings back to a hundred, he hits cruise control. The transport truck catches up, gives another blast on the horn, and passes on the inside lane.

Angela shakes her fist and glares at the driver as he passes. He looks down at her and gives her the finger. Frank loses it. He swears at the disappearing truck and jabs his foot on the accelerator. Nobody utters a peep. We know better than to escalate the situation, especially when Frank is behind the wheel. After a few seconds he eases off the gas and returns to his normal self — whatever that is.

We pass a string of buses labouring up the hill. They're packed with shift workers going to their barracks and their jobs in the oil sands. Then we pass the same transport truck, which is also struggling up the hill. We pull alongside; my stomach is churning.

"Don't, Frank," Angela warns. "He's a lot bigger than us."

Frank waves at the driver, his middle finger raised slightly above the others. Despite the grin on his face, we all know what he means. *Thank god* Frank doesn't see the driver's full-on eff-you gesture as we surge past. *Crap!* What's gonna happen when the road levels off?

We level off.

All thoughts of the truck driver fly out the window.

The landscape looks about as welcoming as the surface of the moon.

My grandfather mumbles something about the treaty. He told me the treaty story many times when I was a kid. He must have told it really well, because the treaty was signed over a hundred years ago — even before *he* was born, yet in my memory I was *there*. Apart from this one major flaw, I'm sure that everything else he said was true. My grandfather's grandfather was one of the men who had talked with the British, although *talked* isn't the right word, because he didn't speak their language, and they didn't speak his. And he couldn't read the letter from Queen Victoria either. Nor could any of the other Chipewyan, Cree, or Métis. But the queen had sent an interpreter, and he explained that she wanted them to live in peace with her British subjects. My ancestors had thought the newcomers were asking for a friendship treaty, like the ones they'd made with other bands and tribes and nations.

A Catholic priest was already working in Fort Chipewyan. "For some crazy reason," my grandfather always said, "the people trusted that black robe. They believed him when he said that our lives would remain more or less unchanged and that we'd still be able to hunt, and trap, and fish, just as we always had. There was a lot of land, and there were very few people, so we agreed to share. We made a spoken promise ... one that was for *as long as the sun shines, as long as the grass grows, as long as the river runs*. We also made our mark on the queen's paper. We didn't know that the scratchy lines said that we agreed to *cede* the land to the queen. We didn't know that *cede* meant *give up; relinquish; hand over*!"

The way my grandfather's story goes, Queen Victoria's representatives gave the people gifts as a sign of her friendship. Chiefs got thirty-two dollars plus a silver medal. My grandfather's grandfather got twenty-two dollars, because he was what they called a *head man*. Everyone else, *Indians* as they called us, got twelve dollars. Whenever my grandfather told the story, it never crossed my mind to ask why they called us Indians. I didn't know back then that Indians come from India. For hundreds of years we've been called Indians because Christopher Columbus was going the wrong way around the world and thought he'd landed in India when he "discovered" America!

Apart from the cash, the queen gave the Indians ammunition for hunting and twine for fishing, as well as hoes, rakes, and shovels. The whole band got a plow and a pair of horses to share. Then she gave the people land. One square mile per family. She called it their reserve. I never got how the queen gave the people land that was theirs in the first place. It didn't seem a fair exchange for two hundred *million* acres that spread from the Northwest Territories across Northern Alberta and into both British Columbia and Saskatchewan. Of course, the people could still use all that land for hunting and fishing as before, except — and this is another phrase from the treaty that my ancestors couldn't read, a phrase that wasn't explained — *except if the land is required for settlement, mining, lumbering, trading, or other purposes.*

I gaze out of the truck window at the landscape that flies past and at the turnoffs for the big names like Suncor and Syncrude and Shell.

For the first time in my life I realize how badly we got screwed.

CHAPTER SEVEN

The fish hawk flies across the barren landscape until it gives way to forest once more. She alights on the top of the tallest tree. She's missing a talon on her right foot, but the remaining three claws curve around the branch, holding her securely as she shakes her plumage into position. She preens her feathers to ensure that each one is airworthy. Then, with her job complete, Three Talons looks around and calls for a mate.

Once we get past the turnoffs to the big oil companies, the traffic on Highway 63 thins.

"We're nearly there," Frank says, taking the exit and driving along a road lined with spruce trees that are all the same height, width, and colour. They remind me of soldiers on parade. He pulls onto the shoulder next to a colossal sign: "ENERGYSE" painted in orange on a blue-green background. It's dazzling compared with the rest of the landscape, which is washed-out and muddy grey. Water trickles over slabs of rock, collecting in a pond next to the sign. Lily pads float there. They must be plastic because it's too early for real ones, but it's impossible to tell for sure because they're covered in the same mud-coloured dust that's everywhere.

My grandfather stares at the water and then turns to me.

"Remember the moose wading into the shallows by the cabin? You'd stuff your knuckles into your mouth, trying to keep quiet, but it never worked for long. You'd explode, and they'd bound away."

I can't remember this, but I don't want to spoil his pleasant memory, so I nod.

But Frank ruins the moment. "Do you want to go back up there, old man? Do you want to be all alone again, with no family, with just the damn moose to keep you company?"

"Frank! Take it easy," Angela says.

"I boarded up the windows the day I left," my grandfather continues, obviously knowing how to tune my father out, "to keep animals from moving in."

Frank chuckles in that mean way of his. "Even the animals wouldn't want to live there. It's such a dump."

"You're such an ass," I mumble.

Frank glances over his shoulder. "What's that, Adam?"

I set my face in a stony stare.

Frank steps on the gas and pulls away from the Energyse sign. But suddenly, my grandfather is unbuckling his seat belt and opening the back door.

"What the hell!" Frank yells, slamming on the brakes. "Get back in!"

But my grandfather is out of the truck, even before it comes to a full stop. I wonder if he's had enough of his own son and if he's planning to walk all the way back up to Fort Chipewyan. In one of those crazy split-second decisions, I figure I'll go with him, and I'm out the door too. But he's not going to Chip. He's going back to the pond by the Energyse sign. And so am I.

He starts climbing the rocks, and I'm right after him. A glance over my shoulder shows that Angela and Frank are on our tail.

My grandfather's face soon falls.

"There's no stream," he says. "Where does the water come from?"

Frank laughs. "Nowhere! They just pump it around in a loop."

"Cool!" I exclaim.

Cars slow down and people stare at us. "Get back in the truck," Frank orders. "Everyone's looking."

The entrance to the mine reminds me of border crossings I've seen on TV — flashing red stoplights and guards. Frank puts his card in the machine, and the bar rises. The guard waves us through. Road signs and instructions point off in all directions, as well as orders such as DO NOT ENTER. Frank doesn't need to read the signs. He knows where he's going.

"It's not this quiet as a rule," he says. "They've timed this tree-planting with a shutdown for maintenance."

"That's convenient," my grandfather mutters. "Visitors won't get to see what goes on around here."

Frank snaps. "Look, Dad, this company pays my wages, remember that. It pays for the roof over our heads and the food that goes in our bellies — yours too."

"There was a time *nobody* had to pay for our food!" my grandfather counters. "We ate real fish and real game, not these hot dogs and hamburgers you call food. We drank water from the lake too, not from plastic bottles."

I don't get my grandfather's point. I really like hotdogs and hamburgers. And pop beats water any day. I stick my earbuds in, trying to drown them out with my music.

Frank drives across the moonscape to a place where massive machinery is parked. I perk up.

"Those are the 797s," Frank says.

"You drive one of those?" I shriek.

He nods. "I told you they were big."

"Big? You're kidding. They're colossal."

"As tall as a two-storey house," he says.

46

"Are they hard to drive?"

"Not really. They have power steering, so they're light and responsive. The hardest part is getting into them. You get a workout climbing up and down that ladder."

"Can you take me for a ride?" I ask.

"I wish I could…."

He pulls away from the monster trucks, and we go up a slope to a place where a crowd is gathering. Frank tells me to leave my iPhone in the car. I don't; I stuff it deep in my pocket. We sit on the tailgate, taking off our shoes and waiting for Frank to hand us each a pair of black rubber boots that he bought from Canadian Tire just for today. I'm not happy about Frank choosing my footwear, but I go along with it since I really don't want to wreck my new kicks.

"Perfect for tree-planting," he says, talking about the boots, "and perfect weather too. Early spring, like this … soil still damp from the melt. It's perfect."

"Just perfect," I say under my breath.

Frank covers his face and neck with bug spray and then hands the aerosol can down the line for us to do the same. You can barely smell the DEET because there's something stronger in the air, like when you drive past a road crew filling potholes, only much more powerful. Then I realize it's the smell of the oil industry: summer road works.

Frank gives us matching red baseball caps too, but there's no way I'm wearing one. They look like freebies from Canadian Tire! I yank my Oilers cap firmly onto my head and stare at him coldly until he looks away. We walk toward the group. *The perfect family.* Frank tosses an arm over my grandfather's shoulder, pulling him close. If you didn't know him, you'd think they actually liked each other, but Frank's quiet voice is tinged with threat. "Watch what you say today, Dad. I know you have strong opinions about the mining, but keep them to yourself … for my sake."

My grandfather looks Frank in the eye and says nothing.

CHAPTER EIGHT

A male fish hawk flies high over the heads of the tree planters. Their eyes are downcast and he passes by, unseen. Like the female with the missing talon, this white-chested male is also returning to the place of his birth for the first time.

Three years earlier, he had been the only surviving juvenile from the summer's brood. When icy winds had gusted through the trees and his parents had flown away from the nest, he followed them. But when they went their separate ways, he shadowed his mother. She had led him on his first migration.

Guided by the curving lifelines of the rivers, mother and son flew south over America's heartland, avoiding the pockets of industrialization where the air was thick. Instead, they flew high above the Great Plains, where gangs of man-machines moved across the brown earth in unnaturally straight lines, leaving clouds of dust in their wake.

Each beat of the young bird's wings had brought him closer to maturity, closer to independence, until he suddenly stopped following his mother and headed out in his own direction.

Before long, the air warmed and tasted of salt. Something told him it was where he was supposed to be. So there, in the solitude of Louisiana's bayous and backwaters, he had made his home.

Two winters passed.

Then the urge to find a mate overcame his need for food and comfort. His wings had a mind of their own, launching him high into the air to carry him back to northern Alberta where he was born. But he did not retrace his original flight path. Instead, he flew westward to the edge of the great mountains, then north alongside them — three thousand miles, over a landscape that he had never seen before, to the place of his birth.

But the place of his birth is nowhere to be found.

Shaded from the spring sunshine by a white canopy, the men in suits say it's a great day, an auspicious day, and one that has been a long time coming. They say it's proof that the company takes its environmental responsibility seriously and that they are proud of this new phase in the oil sands industry. They say that Energyse has been working for many years to reclaim a tailings pond and that all the effort and expense have led to this wonderful day when trees are delivered from the nursery and are planted by hundreds of volunteers. I feel a swell of pride to be included in the process, but then the suits go on … and on … and on. It's boring. I put in my earbuds and pull my hoodie around my neck to hide them.

Finally, the speeches end and each of the suits plants a tiny tree, pausing mid-dig for photo ops. Frank spots my earbuds and glares at me. I glare back, and he turns away, but even over my music I can hear him talking to others.

"I hope these photos get into newspapers across the country," he says. "People need to see that the land is being put back to how it was before the mining started."

I can't imagine that all this bare ground will become forest again with trees as big as the ones we saw on the drive up, but the people here seem to know what they are doing, and obviously reforestation is a priority, so I don't get why my grandfather is so negative about it. I guess he's stuck in his old ways and doesn't want to see anything change, not even when it's for the good of the country.

Having planted their little trees, the suits quickly climb into the limos and take off, leaving us choking on dust. The supervisor is giving us instructions, so I take out my earbuds and listen. He tells us to pair up and work across the land in rows. Frank quickly throws his arm around Angela's shoulder, leaving me to work with my grandfather. None of us would have it any other way. I place each little tree into the shallow hole that my grandfather digs and then use the toe of my boot to gently press the earth back into place around the stem. Apparently the trees with long soft needles are pines, the ones with shorter prickly needles are spruces, and the ones that look like dead twigs are poplars. My grandfather shows me the faintest trace of buds breaking on the stems.

I'm close enough to Frank to hear him telling other tree planters about his role in the mining process and about his haulage truck. "She's not like the trucks you see on construction sites in Edmonton or McMurray. When I stand next to her, my head only reaches halfway up the tire! The power shovels are the only machines on site that are bigger than my baby. They scoop a hundred tons in one bite and dump it in my truck so fast that I barely have time to stop."

There are many things I hate about my father. He can be a real jerk. A total ass! But all the same, I have to admit I'm proud of what he does here. Who wouldn't be impressed by the 797 he drives?

The supervisor checks out the trees that my grandfather and I have just planted. "You're doing a great job," he says. "Do you have any questions?"

I do, but I don't know how to ask them without seeming like an idiot. I thought I'd learned *every-thing* about the extraction of oil from the sands at the recent school trip to the Oil Sands Discovery Centre, but now I realize that I don't even know what tailings are. I must have been thinking about something else that day. I smile at the memory of Chrissie. She was in a different class from me, so we hadn't met at school, not officially, but I'd seen her in my neighbourhood. I even knew where she lived, because I sort of stalked her one day.

When we'd assembled for one of the demonstrations, there was only one guy between us, a short kid from Grade Eight. I elbowed him out of the way until I was standing right next to her, our arms almost touching. She looked at me like I was invading her space, but then she smiled. My bones went soggy, almost too weak to keep me upright. At the time I thought it was love. Now I wonder if it was leukemia.

Despite the Chrissie distraction, I *had* learned a lot on that school trip. A woman spooned greasy black sand into a glass beaker. She poured in boiling water from a kettle, stirred it, and let it rest. Bitumen soon rose to the top. The sand settled to the bottom. And dirty water was in the middle. She told us that the same thing happens in the processing plant, except on a bigger scale. She said that the sand is returned to the open pit mine as part of the reclamation process, and the water is reheated and used for the next batch. Chrissie said that the glob of bitumen, dangling from the Popsicle stick in a thick, goopy strand, looked like stiff molasses. I agreed, even though I had no clue what molasses was. But it was easy to see that the stuff was way too thick to flow through a pipeline. No wonder they have to thin it down. The word they used was *upgrade*.

"Any questions?' the tree-planting supervisor asks again.

Holding a miniature spruce tree in one hand, I raise my other hand and wait, like I'm in school. I feel foolish, bring my hand down fast, and blurt out my question.

"What exactly are tailings?"

"Tailings are the slurry that's left after the oil has been extracted from the sand. We pump it to a tailings pond and leave it a while so that any remaining oil can rise to the top and be skimmed off. Most of the sediment settles out too, so then we can recycle the water for washing more oil sand. Recycling is important. We don't want to use more water from the river than we have to."

The supervisor's explanation sounds fine to me, but I can see that my grandfather is not convinced.

"What happens to the sediment?" he asks.

"That's always been one of our most challenging issues," the supervisor admits. "We want all of the land here to be reclaimed and returned to the province as soon as possible, so we're constantly working on new ways to dispose of tailings safely."

"You mean you haven't been doing it safely for forty years!" my grandfather says.

The supervisor looks ready to bolt for his life, like a startled rabbit. "I'm here to help you plant trees," he says, bravely holding his ground. "Once these babies grow up, the land will be much better than it was before. It was useless back in the day — too wet to do anything with. But we've made it higher and drier."

"Good idea," my grandfather says. "It was only muskeg."

I hear the subtle sarcasm and know my grandfather is pissed off, but the supervisor has no idea! He's proud of his project.

"Soon there'll be hiking trails and lookout points and nesting sites for birds. We're already putting in snags, see." He points to a tree trunk that appears to be growing upside down. The roots are in the sky. I've never seen anything like it.

My grandfather laughs aloud, his humour genuine. "You people really have got things wrong side up."

The supervisor laughs too. "It looks that way, I have to agree! But the roots provide a great platform for bigger birds to build their nests. We're hoping that osprey, maybe even eagles, will make it home. And once the trees have grown up a little, animals will come back. It's already happening over at the East Mine. They have a herd of bison grazing there."

"Wild?" my grandfather asks.

"Not exactly. They're fenced in. We're concerned about overgrazing."

"You mean you let them out now and again for photographs to put in the newspaper," my grandfather says.

I scowl at him, trying to tell him to shut up.

"Fifty years from now," the supervisor says, sweeping his arm across the horizon, "all of this land will be covered with trees, and the area will be productive."

"Productive?" my grandfather queries.

"Yes. It's a great opportunity for the logging industry."

I hear my grandfather's quick intake of breath. "I can't listen to any more of this," he tells me. "Let's walk."

I don't much want to go with him, but it beats planting trees. Frank raises his head as we trudge past. "Don't go far," he warns. "And keep out of the restricted areas."

"Restricted areas? This is the land of my ancestors. How can it be restricted to me and my grandson?"

Frank glares at my grandfather. "I'm serious, Dad. It's dangerous around here. I don't want you and Adam getting into trouble. And I don't want you making me look bad, either."

"Okay, okay," my grandfather replies. "We'll behave!"

CHAPTER NINE

The white-chested male is exhausted. He needs to eat in order to keep searching for his home. He spots a pond. The morning sun bathes it in golden light, convincing him that a shoal of small fish swims just under the sparkling surface. He pins his wings and dives. By the time he realizes his error, it's too late to turn back, and he splashes into the water. He bobs up quickly, flapping his wings to get airborne, as he always does. But this time his wings refuse to lift him more than a few inches from the surface. He struggles, as if carrying a fish more than twice his weight, but his curved talons hold nothing. Barely skimming the surface, he flies in a ragged pattern, his wing tips splashing frantically and his feet paddling wildly, until he reaches the shore. Immediately, he begins teasing his feathers with his beak, trying to clean his plumage, but it doesn't work. The blackness sticks to his beak, and when he tries to rub it off by dragging his head along the ground, it just gets worse.

The white-chested fish hawk is covered in oil.

My grandfather's anger seems to be propelling him faster than usual, and I can barely keep up, which is crazy since I'm a runner and he's fifty-something. I stop at the silver F-350 pickup, Frank's newest baby. The shiny paint that he takes such pride in is covered in a haze of dust. He'll be ticked about that. I smile at the thought and then write WASH ME on the tailgate. When I look up, my grandfather is far ahead. I run after him, following the sign to TAILINGS POND D. The road's not paved. It's dirt, almost identical to everything else around here, except that it's packed down. There aren't any trees, so it's easy to spot the high wire fence ahead. We walk toward it. Silently. It's my grandfather's way.

"Frank is so mean sometimes," I say.

My grandfather sighs, our footsteps falling in unison on the rutted road. "He didn't have the best start in life," he says. "Try to give him a break."

I laugh aloud. "Like you do?"

My grandfather laughs too, briefly. Then his face falls. "Rose went to residential school, you know. It changed her. Bottom line, we didn't do a very good job of raising Frank. He didn't get the love he should have."

I can't imagine my grandfather not being loving to his own son. He's not that way with me. It doesn't make sense. Before I can get to the bottom of it, we reach a gate. It *should* block the road, but it's wide open. A sign says NO ENTRY TO UNAUTHORIZED PERSONNEL.

I grab my grandfather's shoulder as he walks through the opening. "We can't go there!"

He shrugs and keeps walking.

We follow the road up the slope to the brow of the hill and stop dead. A black lake stretches into the distance. We stand and stare, speechless. We don't notice the bird at first. It's well camouflaged in the sludge at the edge of the lake. But then it flaps its wings in a pathetic attempt to fly away. Immediately, my grandfather takes off his plaid jacket and walks toward the bird. It screams, dragging itself along the ground, flailing its enormous sludge-covered wings, trying to get airborne to escape the jacket that sails over its head.

"If it can't see us, it's less likely to panic," my grand-father says, poking the bird's head into one of the sleeves. "And I need to make sure it can't get at me with its beak. It's razor-sharp. It could take my fingers off."

My stomach flips at the thought. "Why can't it fly? Does it have a broken wing?"

"It can't fly because its feathers are stuck together with oil."

"Is it an eagle?"

"I don't think so. It has talons like an eagle, but it's too small."

"It could be a baby eagle," I suggest.

My grandfather shakes his head. "It's a hawk. Probably a fish hawk. Some folks call them osprey. But we won't know for sure until we see the colour of its feathers. Who knows what's under all of this sludge. We'll take it home, clean it up, and then let it go."

"How do we clean it?" I ask.

"I don't know. I've never done this before. We have to do something, though."

My grandfather's enthusiasm suddenly vanishes. "What's your father going to say when we tell him we want to put an oily hawk in his precious new truck?"

A loud boom almost makes us jump out of our skin. Then another and another.

"They're shooting at us!" my grandfather yells. "Run!" He grabs the bundled bird, holding it firmly against his chest.

We race down the embankment, glancing over our shoulders, expecting to see men with rifles chasing us. But no one's there. Once we're through the gate, the noise stops. I'm more shaken up than I'm prepared to admit, even to my grandfather. My heart almost pounds out of my chest! We head back to the car park — fast — only stopping to catch our breath and rewrap the bird so its sharp claws won't rip into my grandfather's chest.

By the time we get to the truck, my grandfather barely has the strength to climb into the flatbed and arrange the bird in a corner. I'm tired too, but I fuss over it for a while, letting in air so the poor thing doesn't suffocate and padding its legs to protect the bed of the truck from the sharp talons.

"What are we going to tell Frank?" I ask.

"Nothing! There's no point in getting into a fight unless we have to. We'll just leave the bird here and wedge it in with the toolbox. Let's hope it keeps quiet. And let's hope your parents finish up soon. This bird's in a bad way."

"I can go fetch them, tell them I'm sick and we need to go home?"

My grandfather scoffs. "Best to tell them that *I'm* sick. That would be more believable. But let's give them ten more minutes."

He sinks into silence, and we wait.

Suddenly he seems to have a light-bulb moment. "It wasn't just chance that you rescued this bird. I called you Hawk when you were a kid, remember?"

I nod. "It's way better than Adam. How come they called me *that*?"

"Frank and Angela didn't have much time to think about a name! You were early — a whole month early — and so little! Nobody thought you'd be around for long. The priest came right away, baptizing you, so that you'd have a place in Heaven."

He shakes his head and gives that little lip-sucking thing of his, telling me, without words, that he has no time for the Catholic faith of my mother.

"They needed to come up with a name straight away, so they called you Adam."

One more reason for me *never* to forgive my parents. They couldn't even be bothered to choose a name for me during the eight months that I lived inside Angela. I can just imagine the priest arriving the day of my birth, baby-name book in hand, opening it to the first page … and there you go … Adam.

"You never looked like an Adam to me," my grandfather continues. "You looked like a bird! A newly hatched one. Scrawny! Arms and legs like twigs! And a mouth that opened wide, looking for food." He opens his mouth and chirps in a fair impression of a baby bird. I can't keep myself from laughing.

"When I held out my hand, you jerked your arms around until you grasped my finger. You held on real tight, like a young fish hawk gripping the side of the nest. That's when I called you Hawk."

"How come you didn't call me Hawk when you moved in with us?"

My grandfather shrugs. "Frank and Angela didn't care for the name. I think it reminded them of their roots, and they wanted to forget all of that. So I called you Adam to keep the peace. In my heart, though, you've always been Hawk." He looks up. "Here they are!"

Frank heads to the tailgate, but my grandfather diverts him.

I tell Angela to sit on the running board so I can help her with her boots, even insisting that I take them to stow in the truck's bed.

"Why are you being so helpful?" she asks.

"I'm not!" I protest.

"Did you hear the cannons?" Frank asks.

"Cannons?" my grandfather and I answer in unison.

"They scare the birds away from the tailings ponds," Frank says.

"Cannons with cannon balls?" I ask.

"No! It's just noise."

"Guess it doesn't work too well," my grandfather says.

"Not as good as the new systems they're developing," Frank says proudly. "Radar detects incoming birds, identifies the species, and makes a sound to deter them."

"What sort of sound?" I ask.

"It depends. If it's a bird that would normally get eaten by a hawk or an eagle, then the machine plays a recording of a hawk or an eagle. That scares the bird off. Neat, eh?"

"What if the *incoming* bird is a hawk or an eagle?"

Frank frowns. "I'm sure they have an answer for that too."

CHAPTER TEN

Again and again, Three Talons calls for a mate. She has yet to experience the sky-dance of courtship, yet somehow she anticipates the moment when a mate will swoop down from the heavens in his dramatic aerial display. He will become her one and only breeding partner. He should have arrived before her. That is the way. He should have already chosen a nesting site for them. That, too, is the way. Innate wisdom tells her that nest-building is futile without him — the nest has a single purpose: a place for her to lay fertile eggs and sit on them long enough for the chicks to hatch and fledge. She calls again. And listens.

There is no reply.

As we get closer to home, my grandfather and I exchange nervous glances. The townhouse in McMurray is much bigger than the old place in Chip, but it's still nowhere near big enough to hide a colossal oil-covered raptor. I imagine carrying the filthy thing to the main bathroom, putting it in the white tub and washing it with Angela's washcloths while it flaps oily black water everywhere and scrapes the paint with its talons. We'd never get away with it. Even the laundry tub is white, so that's not an option either. I washed my muddy running shoes there once, so I know how much trouble I'd get into. I'm starting to think that we should just come clean and tell Frank and Angela about the bird, but I'm scared that Frank might stop the truck and toss the poor thing out.

My grandfather leans over and whispers in my ear. "Ask that googley thing of yours how to clean oil off birds."

"Dawn dish detergent," I whisper back a few moments later.

"Do we have Dawn?"

I shrug. "Don't think so. I think it's Dove."

My grandfather chuckles. "Dove? You're kidding, right? Dove — for a hawk! Sounds perfect."

By the time we reach the suburbs of McMurray and pull into the garage, my grandfather has a plan, and he whispers one simple instruction. "Get the Dove."

Unfortunately, Angela is heading into the kitchen just as I am sneaking out with the bottle shoved under my T-shirt.

"Adam! What have you got there?"

I show her the soap. "I was just going to … er … wash my bike in the garage."

Angela rolls her eyes. "Can't you do better than that? What's going on?"

"Promise you won't tell Frank."

"He's already asleep. He was tired from the driving. I won't tell him."

I blurt out the whole story.

"How can I help? What do you need?"

"*Wow!*" I say. "Warm water to soften the oil."

"Connect the garden hose to the tap in the laundry room and pass it through the window."

My grandfather comes into the kitchen. "Make it quick," he whispers. "The bird's not doing well."

He sees Angela and stops in his tracks.

"She knows," I explain, "but it's okay. She's gonna help."

He looks as surprised and relieved as I was. "We have to hurry. The bird's not going to last much longer."

"Are we doing this in the backyard?" Angela asks.

"The oil scum will kill the grass," my grandfather replies.

"How about the driveway?" Angela suggests. "The water can run down to the road and go into the storm sewer."

"The whole neighbourhood will see!"

She shrugs. "Maybe the whole neighbourhood needs to see."

By the time I have everything set up, my grandfather has already taped the bird's beak shut, taking care not to cover its nostrils.

"I was going to tape its legs too," he says, "but it's almost dead — I doubt it will struggle. In fact, I doubt it will survive the washing, let alone try to fly away."

My grandfather and I take turns rubbing liquid soap into the feathers while Angela rinses away the brown bubbles with a gentle stream of warm water. Cars slow down to see what's going on. Neighbours walk over.

White plumage emerges on top of the bird's head.

"It's a bald eagle!" a girl exclaims.

I turn toward the voice. It's Chrissie! She's front and centre of a crowd that has gathered unnoticed.

"Bald eagles are bigger," I announce. *Crap! I sound like a know-it-all.*

"I think this is a fish hawk," my grandfather states. A few moments later the bird's white breast feathers and long white legs emerge from the dirt. "An osprey — just as I thought — a male."

"How do you know?" Chrissie asks.

"Males are smaller than females," my grandfather says. "This one's not that big."

Chrissie gasps. "Not that big! I've never seen such a big bird in my life"

My grandfather smiles. "There's another way to tell. The females have brown flecks around their throat, like a necklace. This one has dark smudges here and there, but it's oil, not plumage. He's gonna have a nice white throat when he's all cleaned up. It'll match his chest and legs.

The scum heading toward the gutter is almost white, so Angela does one long and final rinse, and then my grandfather wraps the bird in a bath towel and carries it through to the backyard. The crowd follows, people squeezing in against the back wall of the house, everyone trying to give the bird as much space as possible. My grandfather sets it gently on the grass and untapes its beak. Then, asking people to stand back, he finally removes the towel.

Nothing happens. The bird sits on the grass, motionless, its legs tucked under its body. The moment is anticlimactic. A few people get bored and leave, but most stay, some even praying. Suddenly the bird stands and shakes its enormous wings, shedding the last traces of water. But it soon collapses back onto the grass, looking more dead than alive. Someone brings breaded fish sticks. Someone else brings water. But the bird won't eat or drink.

"D'you think he's gonna make it?" I ask.

"I don't know," my grandfather replies. "It's almost dark. He should be flying into the treetops to roost for the night. If he stays here, he might get eaten by a coyote or attacked by a dog."

"We could put it in my garden shed," Chrissie suggests. "I'm down the street and around the corner, number seventy-nine."

I almost blurt out, "I know," but I catch the words just in time.

"Let's give him a few more minutes," my grandfather says.

Between the houses, the sun slips beneath the horizon, turning the clouds orange. Suddenly the fish hawk stands tall, extending his long legs and flapping his wings furiously. I'm really close to him, closer than anyone else, so I get the frantic wing-beats right in my face, like I'm standing in front of a very big and noisy fan. I duck and step back, bumping into Chrissie! She's ducked low, her arms over her head. Briefly her closeness distracts me, but then the bird springs into the air. He seemed big before, but now, with wings extended, he's colossal. I didn't know birds came in this size — like prehistoric!

In one strong flap, he flies over the fence and lands on the pine tree in the neighbour's yard. The bough bends under his weight. He stays for a few seconds, adjusting his wings and talons to the tight space, and then he tips his head sideways, gazes up, and jumps. The short flight takes him to another perch, closer to the top of the tree. As the light fades, he tucks his head under his wing and becomes invisible.

My grandfather breathes an enormous sigh of relief. "He'll be safe like that tonight."

The crowd disperses, everyone wishing the bird well and congratulating us on a job well done.

Chrissie is the last person to leave. "I'm Chrissie," she tells me.

I pretend that I don't already know.

"And that was really, really cool. See you around."

"Yeah, see you later," I say, trying to keep my voice low and husky. It doesn't work. There's a squeak at the end, which happens a lot these days when I get nervous. I feel a blush spread across my face. *Damn it!*

"Did that oily bird just drop onto our driveway?" Frank asks the instant we walk back into the kitchen.

"Er ... um ..." I begin, wondering how much of the evening's events he has seen.

"No! It didn't just drop onto our driveway," my grandfather says, his neck flushed and his voice loaded with scorn. "We found it. Guess where? Tailings Pond D! You know the place, eh?"

"So you brought it home in my truck?" Frank says, ready to explode.

"Yes!" my grandfather replies, growing stronger with this single powerful word.

"My *new* truck?"

Frank is really pissed, but he's keeping a lid on it ... so far. Then he turns to sarcasm, one of his ugly ways of fighting. "I'm surprised you didn't put the damn thing on the front seat and tell it to buckle up."

I hate him!

"You!" he says, pointing at me. "Get back out there and clean every trace of oil from my flatbed. And if there are scratch marks —"

He doesn't finish the threat! He turns and walks away! I'm stunned that I got off so easy, but my grandfather doesn't get that we should quit while we're ahead. He's generally so quiet and wise, but this has him riled up, and he won't drop it.

"So what are you going to do about Tailings Pond D?" he demands loudly.

Frank strides back and meets my grandfather head on. I seriously wonder if there's going to be a fist-fight. My poor old grandfather wouldn't stand a chance. Fortunately, Frank contains his anger. "What do you think this is, Dad? I'm not management!"

My grandfather is in no mood for excuses. "Those tailings ponds are killing birds! God knows what else they're killing. *You* work there! *You* should do something."

"For god's sake, Dad, I already told you, I don't run the company."

"You should still be able to do *something*."

"It's just a few birds!" Frank shouts. "Don't get so uptight."

My grandfather gives Frank a dismissive wave and heads off to bed. I breathe a sigh of relief and trudge back out to clean the truck.

I wake early and race into the yard in my boxers, but the white-chested fish hawk is gone. I'm happy, but I'm really sad too.

CHAPTER ELEVEN

Three Talons calls as she rides the thermals, her long wings widely stretched, the tips of her feathers merely fluttering. In spiralling circles she increases her range northward, her bright yellow eyes taking in every detail, until finally, on the shifting wind, she hears a reply. She alights on a tree limb and waits. The calls become louder until a male osprey lands on the branch next to her, but his soapy scent smells wrong. She screeches her objections, driving him away. From high above her, he calls, and in his voice she hears the language of her kind. It's enough. She preens her ruffled feathers while he demonstrates his prowess in flight by swooping past her in a blur. She's impressed.

I've been pretending that I'm not here in this hospital. I've escaped for a few hours by reliving events in the past, but the reality is I'm still here. And I'm not going anywhere any time soon.

Frank's medical insurance will pay for a private room for me, but Angela says it's *not* a good idea for me to be alone. She thinks I need the company of other young people. I can't stand the thought. I'm sure that most of the other patients feel the same way. Their turned-away faces and lowered eyes say *leave me alone.* A boy called Leon, however, seems determined to make me his new best friend. Despite his bald head and grey skin, he seems brighter and more upbeat than you'd expect. I watch him work his magic on the others. He doesn't quite get them rolling in the aisles, but at least he gets a smile or sometimes a laugh. Not me, though. I don't want to smile. I don't want to laugh. And I don't want a new best friend. I want to be alone. I beg for the privacy of my own room. Frank and Angela rarely say *No* to me, so when Angela fights me on this I'm surprised. But eventually I win. After all, who can say no to Cancer Boy?

So I don't have to lie around any more, worrying about when I'll turn into a bald-headed stick-person like the rest of them. I can watch TV any time I want, and if I feel like talking, there's a steady stream of adults willing to pass the time of day. The doctors and nurses are really good at explaining things. They've given me a new understanding of the human body. I never knew that even if we live to be eighty, most of our individual cells don't live very long at all. New cells are born, do their job, get tired, and die. The number of dying cells usually equals the number of cells being born, so everything stays in balance. It's easy to see this happening with our skin. A summer tan fades because the old tanned cells wear off and get replaced with new ones. Cuts heal. Scars disappear. But deep inside our bodies, the same thing happens. Even broken bones grow back together. To me this sounds about as crazy as getting your car all dinged up, but instead of taking it to the body shop, you just leave it. Two months later, your ride looks as if it's just come from the showroom, like an invisible repairman has been lovingly filling dents and painting them over.

The problem with cancer is that the repairman can't stop filling the dent. He's obsessed! He keeps going and going, slapping on more and more filler until the dent becomes a lump: a tumour. People with leukemia don't get tumours though, because the cancer is in our white blood cells, and they're continually hurtling through veins and arteries. They never slow down enough for the cancer cells to clump. I suppose it's like the repairman filling dents in the pouring rain — the filler keeps getting washed away.

But there's one thing that I still don't get. White blood cells are *good*. They fight infection, like soldiers in a war on germs, and they clean up dead and dying stuff, like garbage collectors. You'd think that having more of them would give me super clean blood and make me super healthy. I'm obviously missing a piece of the puzzle.

Noticing my interest in all things cancer-related, Angela suggests that instead of being a chemical engineer in the oil industry, which was her previous goal for my life, I should become a doctor.

"That's assuming I live long enough to do either," I tell her.

"You will!" she states firmly.

"You don't know that," I shout, my mood turning ugly so fast that it shocks even me. "You're not God! You said everything was going to be okay, but it's not."

I see heartache on her face, but I keep going, pushing the knife deeper and turning it. "It's *not* okay. And it's not *going* to be okay. You were *wrong* about the growing pains too. You were *wrong* about putting me in the same wards as all those other losers. You're *always* wrong."

Letting off steam helps me. It doesn't help Angela, but that's not my problem. I push the guilt away. She deserves everything I give her and more. However, it doesn't take long for remorse to sneak in. Angela is being nice, and I really am glad she's with me, because it would be far worse if I was alone. But I can't bring myself to say that out loud.

When the anger fades, I realize that the kids in Ward C are no more losers than I am.

CHAPTER TWELVE

Despite the unrecognizable landscape, the two birds find it hard to leave the area. Instinct still tells them that this is home, so they choose a tree that is as close to their birthplace as they dare go. The tree is dying, but it's what they prefer. With their large wingspan, they need a nest they can swoop in and out of without getting snagged on dense branches and needles. White Chest makes the decision as to the exact location of the nest and immediately starts bringing branches and twigs for the framework. But Three Talons is fussy. She makes several false starts, pushing the branches around and tweaking them with her beak. Then she abandons her efforts and takes to the air, screeching as if complaining that nothing is as good as her old home.

White Chest searches out another tree. He finds one that will perfectly support the enormous platform of nesting material. It's farther from the river than before, so they will have to spend more time and energy flying back and forth with food for the family, but ancient knowledge tells them to make a decision fast ... build a nest ... start a family.

The days are still growing longer....

But the birds know that time is growing short.

I'm getting closer to figuring out leukemia.

I've learned that *all* blood cells are made in the bone marrow, which is the spongy centre of my bones. I imagine my bone marrow as a car manufacturing plant — say like Ford — building SUVs, minivans, and pickups, like Frank's. The boss knows how many of each to get on the production line, based on what customers are ordering. But if the boss goes on work-to-rule, the order gets messed up, and a few lemons probably slip through. Switching that analogy to my bone marrow factory ... the boss has gone on strike, and in the chaos, I get way too many white cells and not enough red cells or platelets. To make matters worse, these white cells never grow into fully functioning adults. They're lemons! They just hang around doing nothing, not even taking out the garbage, which is one of their main jobs. This amuses Angela, who mutters know-it-all comments about helpless children and lazy teenagers. *What does she know?*

Before I got leukemia, if I got a cut, platelets would throw themselves across the wound, preventing blood from leaking out, sort of like a few sheets of paper towel. But now I don't have enough platelets, so I bleed —

From my gums when I brush too hard or eat raw food —

From my nose when I breathe too hard —

And under my skin, when the tiniest little bang gives me a huge bruise.

And because I don't have enough *red* blood cells to carry oxygen around my body, I'm constantly exhausted.

Now that I've got a handle on all of that, it's easier to understand the treatment. It comes down to this: They start by knocking me out to put a central line straight into the big vein that leads into my heart. This means that they don't have to keep poking me with a needle every time they want to push drugs into me. With my shortage of platelets and the tendency to bleed, a constant barrage of needles would be a little counter-productive. Then they'll drip in toxic chemicals. My heart will pump the drugs around my body, killing almost all of the cells in my bloodstream, good and bad. This will make me feel like total crap. It will also almost kill *me*, along with the cancer cells.

Then they'll give me time to recover, hoping that the boss in the bone marrow factory gets back on the job, although I don't know why he should — they don't seem to be offering him any incentive. Hopefully the doctors understand all of this better than I do. They'll monitor my blood, and as soon as I have enough normal cells again, which will be the same time that I begin to feel better, they'll repeat the whole process. More barfing, more feeling like shit, more actual shit! And they'll do this over and over, on and off, for more than three years. I won't be in the hospital the whole time. I'll go back and forth to home and the Northern Lights Hospital in McMurray. But unfortunately, the chemo doesn't always work, hence the 10 percent failure rate. I wonder if it's the cancer that kills us, or if it's the treatment.

Still, no other options are presented. This is it.

CHAPTER THIRTEEN

White Chest works relentlessly, making a sturdy frame of branches and twigs, wrestling them into place with his powerful beak and talons. Then he gathers softer material for Three Talons to arrange. Old, frayed rope, dried grass, coarse wolf hair, and soft fur of the wood buffalo make the nest complete.

Over the next week, Three Talons lays three creamy brown eggs, each with reddish-brown specks. Her hooked beak is strong enough to rip apart a fish, yet she uses it tenderly to turn the fragile eggs under her body, rotating them carefully so that each developing embryo gets its share of her warmth. White Chest delivers whole fish to her, settling on the platform for a while and then heading out again on another fishing expedition. He knows he must feed Three Talons so that she can devote herself to keeping the eggs warm and protecting them from a surprise attack by an eagle or an owl. Without two parents, the young would not survive.

I have a fever. I ache. I feel as if I'm swooping through the air. Angela rubs my back as I dry heave into the kidney bowl. I know I'll lose my hair soon. It's a side effect of the chemotherapy. I've been telling myself that it's only hair and that it will grow back, but in my heart I'm really sad.

Between bouts of puking, Angela suggests that instead of waiting for my hair to fall out in chunks, I have it shaved now. I agree, so she calls the hospital hairdresser. I get into the shower and wash my hair for the final time.

I can feel that I'm about to cry. I tell myself to man up. Self-talk has worked in the past, preparing me for a race or pushing me to make those final hard strides. But hidden in the bathroom and muffled by the sound of running water, I give myself a break — I feel sorry for myself. To my horror, as soon as I give an inch, my emotions get the upper hand and go the whole mile. I'm too exhausted to fight the feelings. I sob from deep inside me, from a place I didn't even know I had. Tears run down the drain with the water. I'm glad that no one can see them. They finally stop falling, and I feel ready to move on.

The hairdresser plugs in the electric clipper and starts to buzz over my head. I laugh and make light of the whole thing, but I feel naked, embarrassed, and incredibly sad. When she's done, I can't stop running my hand over my head. My bathroom doesn't have a mirror, so I sneak into the visitors' bathroom to take a look at myself. A stranger stares back at me. My scalp is a few shades lighter than my face, and it gleams through the stubbly black layer. There are depressions and lumps and bumps in my skull that I never realized were hiding there, and without hair to offer some coverage, I notice that my ears stick out, making me look like a cartoon version of my former self. I keep pressing them in, but they don't stay put. I feel like a foreigner in my own body. It's soul-destroying.

Angela kisses the top of my head and says that I'm handsome, and that my eyes are enormous and look as soft as a deer's.

I haven't seen deer since I lived in Chip with my grandfather. We'd spot them occasionally, or they would spot us and bound away, white tails raised like flags. But sometimes they would come close to our the cabin, peeking cautiously out of the bush, waiting, watching, and then taking timid steps across the narrow strip of sand to drink from the lake. Across the distance of time, I see thick eyelashes framing huge brown eyes. I can't imagine that Angela sees such beauty in my eyes. She must just be trying to make me feel better.

Three Talons cocks her head, listening for the faint tapping of beaks from inside the shells or for the chirps that indicate they are hatching. After five weeks, her

efforts are rewarded. She has three down-covered, helpless chicks demanding to be fed. White Chest hunts from dawn until dusk, catching fish for his family. Summer is short this far north, and the change in day length drives him to make up for lost time. The young must lose their soft baby fluff and grow flight feathers before they can leave the nest. Even then, they will need more time before they will be independent. They must learn to fly and catch fish. They must grow strong enough to make the long migration to the Gulf Coast before winter sweeps into Alberta.

There is little time.

A hospital volunteer comes into the room. "It's three o'clock," she announces cheerfully. "Snack time!"

Three o'clock makes me think of the end of the school day. It makes me think of Chrissie. It's the day after I get my diagnosis, and she's cycling past my house on the way home from Mercredi High. A baseball cap on backwards keeps her long, sandy hair off her forehead, and as she pumps the pedals, all I can think about is her long, touchable legs. She stares right through the window. Instead of waving to her, I cringe into the shadows of the room, hoping she won't see me.

I wonder what she was thinking as she glanced in my window that day. Was she relieved that we never hooked up? It had been so close. Just a few days before my diagnosis, I'd leaned against her locker and we'd talked. It wasn't as difficult as I'd imagined — we had the oil-covered osprey as a starting point. I suggested we get together on the weekend, and without pausing, she said maybe we could bike ride on the Birchwood Trails and even do some bird watching. *Bird watching? What's with that?* But the thought of being with Chrissie in the woods had driven away all of my fatigue, and I nodded enthusiastically.

None of it matters anymore. Chrissie will never be my girlfriend now. Even worse, I will probably never have a girlfriend — period. It's hard to take in. What if I'm the one out of the ten? I try to imagine the future without myself in it. I can't.

I wonder if Chrissie went bike riding with someone else that weekend. The thought makes me feel left out, like I'm a kid who didn't get invited to a birthday party. But *this* hurts more because I'm not being left out of a stupid party — I'm being left out of *life*! Everyone else is getting on with theirs.

And I'm derailed here.

CHAPTER FOURTEEN

The three osprey chicks are growing fast. The tips of adult feathers poke through ragged baby fluff, unfurling like leaves in the spring and turning the chicks into juveniles who preen themselves with their sharp beaks. Before long, the youngsters are almost the size of their parents. They grasp the edge of the nest with their curved talons and exercise their flight muscles by furiously flapping their growing wings. But it will be another week or more before they have the strength to fly.

Man-machines come.

They roar and belch fiery breath.

White Chest takes to the air and circles overhead, screaming at them. He dives low, trying to drive the enemy away from his family. But the machines keep coming.

The big logging machines are making so much noise that the operators don't hear the birds' distressed cries. They lumber closer. The man in the cab of the first machine focuses on the trunk of the tree he is harvesting, his hands busy with the controls. Metal claws grasp the trunk, holding it firmly as the saw blade cuts it through. He pushes the lever to swing the trunk horizontal, but it's snagged on the neighbouring tree. He looks up and sees an osprey circling overhead. Scanning the treetops, he spots the nest. It's at least six feet across. He knows that there are rules about cutting trees where certain birds are nesting, so he checks his list; osprey nests are to be left undisturbed until after the young birds have fledged. He radios his boss in the other machine to let him know.

"The nest is empty," the boss tells him, yelling into the headset to make himself heard over the machinery.

"I don't think so," the man in the logging machine says. "I can see birds sitting up there."

"They should have fledged by now," the boss replies. "The rules say we have to wait until then, but after that it's fair game. We'd never get any work done around here if we waited for every freakin' bird to leave the nest."

"But they're ospreys!" the man exclaims. "Aren't they on the endangered list?"

The radio crackles while the boss checks his data.

"No! They were once … after DDT killed a lot of them. But they recovered. They're not on the list anymore. But hold on a moment, I'm going to take a look with the binoculars."

The man in the logging machine waits.

The radio crackles again. "They've got their adult plumage. They're old enough to fly. They'll take off as soon as you get close. Keep cutting."

Three Talons stays with her offspring as long as she dares. The machines lumber closer. The noise is terrifying, but she stays … until the forest starts to fall around her. Then she abandons the nest, driven by the need to survive. She and White Chest fly a safe distance away and watch from the treetops. A man-machine grabs the trunk of the tree that holds their family. It bites into the trunk and throws it down, tossing the young birds out. They flap helplessly as they plummet to the ground. The angry man-machine doesn't stop. It keeps eating its way through the forest, leaving a mess of branches … and three young fish hawks trampled into the ground.

CHAPTER FIFTEEN

I made it through my first round of chemotherapy, and I'm back in the ward with the *not-so-sick* kids. I got bumped from my private room because the hospital needed it for someone sicker than me. I was pissed, but Angela says it's good — it means I'm getting better and that *if* things go well, I'll be able to go home for a while. *If* is a very short word, but it's fully loaded.

The patients in Ward C have changed, but so have I.

I'm one of the bald, frail ones now. Even my eyebrows are gone. The newbies still have hair and look more robust, like they could maybe stand up in a breeze. I don't make eye contact with them because I don't want to see the expressions on their faces that say, *Oh, crap! Is that going to happen to me?*

I recognize the guy in the bed next to me from my first stay in this ward. Leon. He was totally bald then, but now he has fine fuzz over his head. It's so blond that it's almost white. And his skin is so pale that it's almost transparent.

He says hi with a toothy grin, his blue-grey eyes shining at me like a couple of pocket flashlights. Before I know what's happening, I've broken my own rules and am talking to him. And I'm happier! I'd never tell Angela she was right, but she *was* — just this once. She doesn't gloat or say I told you so, but I can tell she's happier too. She isn't glued to my side, 24/7. She just comes during visiting hours.

Leon has a sense of humour, finding something to laugh about even in our crappy situation. He makes my mood lighter. Even if I'm having a really bad day or I'm too exhausted to speak, the fact that Leon is there seems to help. When he goes for tests, I miss him. And when I go for tests, it's good to come back and see his familiar face, or his sleeping form under the covers. When he's not around, I'm not the only one to miss him. He's become the key patient in Ward C, effortlessly entertaining us troops with his morale-building humour.

Leon's personality is way bigger than the frail body he lives in. He has no hair to speak of and no accessories, but he still has "it." He charms the nurses, who always stay much longer than necessary when they come to take his vitals, and he convinces the interns to sneak in contraband goodies, such as the 7-Eleven blue raspberry slushie that he is currently downing.

I tell him about my passion for running. He understands. He's obsessed with baseball in the same way.

"When I was a kid, I wanted to be a professional," he says, offering me a slurp of his slushie, "but these days I think I'll study drama. I've been in school plays since I was in kindergarten. I had a lead role last year. Even if I can't play baseball, I should be able to act. At the very least I could play a cancer patient."

I'm amazed that Leon still has a plan for his life and even more surprised that he *had* a plan in the first place.

"I've never had a long-term plan," I tell him. "The only goal I ever set for myself was to win the cross-country competition in McMurray and then the Wood Buffalo Regionals. I saw myself with the gold medal around my neck, standing on the podium, like in the Olympics."

Leon immediately bursts into song, "O Canada —"

I laugh, but as soon as Leon stops singing, *poor me* gushes right back to the surface. "Leukemia put an end to all that."

Leon sighs. "It's hard letting go of dreams, isn't it?"

"It doesn't bother me these days," I lie. "After all, losing the chance at a gold medal is nothing compared to what I stand to lose now."

Leon nods. "Most of the time, I get it — at least I *think* I get it. I mean I've thought about all the possibilities and I understand. But then out of nowhere, none of this seems real, and I say, *No! No way! This isn't happening to me.*"

I look into Leon's eyes. Angela has always said the eyes are the window to the soul. She's right. "Yeah," I say. "That happens to me too."

CHAPTER SIXTEEN

The bond between Three Talons and White Chest is strong and will last until one of them dies. Yet despite this loyalty and devotion, the pair spends the winters apart, instinct driving them from their breeding site in northern Alberta and guiding them south on separate paths. Three Talons wings toward the coastal marshes of Texas, and White Chest flies farther east to the warm bayous of the Mississippi Delta. They hunt and fish in solitude and seclusion, roosting in trees and having no need for a nest. For more than six months they will not see each other. They rarely even see another of their own species.

Angela used up her vacation time and compassionate leave sitting around in the hospital with me, and since my grandfather is stuck in the house in McMurray with nothing to do, they decided to switch. Angela has gone back to work, and my grandfather is coming to take her place. Just as I was beginning to feel more comfortable around my mother, she's gone again. Typical.

I have mixed feelings about my grandfather coming here. If I'm honest with myself, I have to admit that I'm embarrassed by him. His greying hair tied in a ponytail, his clothes, his lack of expression, even his tone of voice … all these things scream First Nations. I left that image behind when I moved to McMurray. So did Frank and Angela. I wonder if people here in the hospital will look at me differently after he gets here.

My grandfather walks purposefully toward me, head high. My heart warms at the sight of him. He says one word in greeting, "Hawk!" And instantly I feel safe, or at least safer.

"Hawk?" I ask.

"You're Hawk from now on, even if Frank and Angela are around. And every time you hear your name, remember that the hawk is strong and courageous, and he has the most powerful eyes of all the creatures. He can see everything from a great height. But he has *vision* too!"

"What's the difference?"

"From high in the sky he sees the fish that he plans to catch, but he sees the bigger picture and takes it all in. He knows when to dive and when to sit it out. There's wisdom in that. He's loyal too. And brave — just like you."

I laugh. "Are you kidding? Look at me!"

"It wasn't just coincidence we found that fish hawk in the tailings pond. *You* helped him, and now *he* will help you."

"How can he help me?"

"He will give you his vision and his courage."

"I'll settle for courage," I say, closing my eyes and reaching for just a glimmer of it in the darkness. Nothing changes. I'm still scared.

"It will come — when you need it most. You'll grow into your name, believe me."

Anger comes out of nowhere. "You're wrong! I will *never* grow into my name, even if I have all the time in the world to do it. And I probably don't."

He rests his hand on mine, and I start to feel safe again. I don't care if other people look down on him. Or me. I'm glad he's here. I relax, like I'm under a spell, and soon I feel myself slipping into a peaceful sleep.

I'm on an old game trail, running. But I'm weightless, as if I have wings on my feet. I hold out my arms, inviting the wind to lift me, and instantly I'm carried into the sky, soaring effortlessly over the forest. My eyesight is superb. I can see for miles. And without even looking at my talons, I know that I'm a fish hawk.

From high in the sky, I see man-machines scurrying around the brown land, devouring the trees and ripping up the earth until no living thing remains. I fly on to where a huge man-machine eats earth, spitting it into another man-machine, like a bird feeding a chick. A flash of human wisdom comes to me: this is where Frank works. I'm watching *his* haulage truck, the 797 he's so proud of. *He's* at the wheel. He revs the engine, and with his load of tar sand spilling over, he drives the rumbling truck away. I let him go.

I angle my wings and follow the great river that flows through the barren land. I see lakes and ponds where fish might dart, where ducks might swim, where hawks might feed. Wanting to rest my weary body and restore my flagging spirit, I fly toward the water, but a voice orders me to stay away, saying that *all* of these ponds and lakes are places of death.

I wake up. My grandfather's hand is still resting on mine.

I tell him about the dream. He smiles. "I told you that the hawk would give you his vision."

I feel a jolt in my chest but brush it off with a laugh. "I wanted courage, not vision."

"Vision comes first."

CHAPTER SEVENTEEN

My grandfather doesn't stay with me 24/7, but he's always there when I need him. It's like he has a sixth sense about these things. In the time alone, Leon and I have become friends. I feel as if I've known him my whole life. We talk about the things that we miss most. Before I got leukemia, girls were high on my list of priorities — Chrissie, at least. It's easy for me to admit this to Leon. And it's good to know that girls were also Number One on his list. Leon is further ahead than I am, though. Before he got cancer, he was dating. But his girl, Melissa, hasn't come to visit him in the hospital. He doesn't expect her to. She lives hours away in Grand Prairie. He tells me all about her ... how crazy beautiful she is, how super smart, how awesomely talented, how hilariously funny. How she's his soul mate.

I tell Leon about Chrissie, and how much I liked her ... *like* her. But that I got sick before anything happened. I didn't even get a kiss. "What are my chances now?" I ask.

"Look around!" Leon says. "You're surrounded by half-naked girls!"

My jaw drops. "You're not serious?"

"I'm just saying," he says.

Although we both laugh, I wonder if my only chance of getting a girlfriend *is* to find someone in the cancer ward, someone who has no other options. We'd be a pair of losers together. Two out of ten.

Without exchanging words, Leon is on the same wavelength. He grabs a math textbook from his nightstand and lets it fall open on his lap. Changing his voice to a husky whisper, he pretends to read. "She looks up at him, eyes misty, lips moist …"

I can't help but laugh.

"Her oxygen tank nestles at their feet. She slips off her mask and their lips meet. For one glorious second, they taste each other. Her heart races. Her breath is ragged. Is it love?"

"No!" I reply. "She needs oxygen."

We both burst out laughing. It feels good.

I take over the storyline. "Their IV stands watch over them as they embrace…."

I pause, struggling to think of something funny. I'm not as good at this as Leon. He picks up.

"Their bodies move gently … his fingers searching hesitantly for a safe place to touch … between her main line, her tubes, and her catheter."

"Let's add a missing limb," I suggest, silliness bubbling up in me.

"You can't *add* a missing limb," Leon says.

"We can add an artificial one."

Leon turns away from me and pulls the sheets over his head. "I'm tired."

Leon takes a couple of days to get back on form. Then he's back at it, befriending the entire world, high-fiving total strangers who come within range and entertaining younger kids who often sneak onto his bed when the nurses aren't looking. He has one of those red clown noses. He whips it out at the most inappropriate moments, which of course turn out to be perfectly timed because the little kids giggle, forgetting, for a few moments at least, that they're horribly sick. Then, when he crosses his eyes as well, they roll around in laughter.

"You'll make a great actor," I tell him. "Just make sure you do comedy."

"You don't think I can do Shakespeare?" he asks, pretending to be hurt. With red clown nose slipping sideways, he stretches out his hand and dramatically grasps at thin air. "Is this a dagger that I see before me?"

His serious face and voice are so at odds with the red nose and crossed eyes that soon I'm rolling around like one of the little kids.

"Can I share your grandfather?" he asks, when I stop laughing. "I don't have one of my own."

"Sure, man, we can be family … cousins or whatever."

Leon immediately starts calling me Cuz and my grandfather Gramps. When Gramps is told about this on his next visit, he responds by dragging his chair between our beds so that Leon and I can share him! Since my grandfather is usually a man of few words, and Leon is rarely at a loss for words, the arrangement works well. When Leon's mom comes to visit and he goes off with her, we both miss him!

An intern drops by, asking where I grew up, what I ate and drank, and if anyone else in my family was sick. Fortunately, my grandfather is able to answer all her questions. Then she invites my grandfather to go off and talk with her some more.

"Why didn't they ask *me* anything?" Leon says.

"Maybe because you aren't First Nations," I tell him.

"That's racist," he says.

I think he's serious until I see the trace of a twinkle in his eyes.

"I've gotta hand it to you, Leon, you're the happiest cancer kid ever."

My grandfather returns. He's sad and angry rolled into one. "I knew years ago that there was something wrong with the fish, but I never put two and two together. I wish I'd trusted my gut."

"What are you talking about?" I ask.

"That intern — she's looking for a connection between the oil sands industry and people getting sick downstream."

"You mean my leukemia could be because of the oil sands?"

"She didn't say that. In fact, she said exactly what your father has always said, that young people all over the world get leukemia, so it's hard to show it has anything to do with the industry. But bile-duct cancer — that's a different matter. She says it's so rare that some doctors never see a single case in their whole career. Yet quite a few people have died from it in Chip. That's what killed your grandmother. I'm sure of it now."

For once in his life, Leon seems to be genuinely serious. "How could she have gotten bile-duct cancer from the oil sands? The industry's miles away."

"Yes, but the Athabasca River flows right through the middle of the oil sands," my grandfather says, "then on into Lake Athabasca."

Leon's jaw drops. "Seriously, the river flows through the oil sands, then right to your front door?"

I nod. "Where I was born, and where I grew up."

"Then how can they possibly say your leukemia has nothing to do with the industry? They're lying, cuz!"

My grandfather doesn't seem to be listening. He's caught up in his own memories. "We never ate the fish that looked off-colour," he says, as if defending himself against an invisible attack. "We only ate the ones that looked okay."

"Looks can be deceiving," Leon mumbles. A flash of understanding goes through me … Leon's humour hides a lot of pain.

My grandfather is still in his own head. "We drank the water from the lake. No one told us not to. We ate roots and herbs and berries that grew near the water. And we ate ducks and geese. A lot of muskrat too, back before they vanished. And beaver. Now they tell us not to eat *any* of these things: none of the country foods that our people have lived on since time began! Especially not organ meat, things like liver and kidney. Rose loved liver. Duck liver was her favourite. Moose liver too. I always gave her my share. Maybe that's why she got cancer and I didn't."

I type "bile-duct cancer Fort Chipewyan" into my iPad. A photo comes up: John O'Connor, a family doctor, the first person to tell the world about high rates of cancer in Chip. The whistle-blower!

"Well, look at that!" my grandfather says. "It's John. He doesn't look a day older."

I look at the date on the photo. It was taken fifteen years ago. "You actually *know* him?"

"Yes, of course I know him. Everyone back in Chip knows him. He started working up there soon after Rose died."

"I didn't think Chip had a doctor!"

"We didn't. Not full-time. John flew in once a month. Nothing's changed. There are so many sick people in Chip, yet we still only have a fly-in doctor. But it's maybe a couple of days a month now."

"*Oh my god*, Gramps. What do people do if they need a doctor?"

"We wait. Or we die!"

"That's wrong," Leon says.

My grandfather shrugs. "We're used to it. But John O'Connor really cared about us. He realized people were getting sick and he went public with it … asked for an investigation. But it didn't do him much good. Or us. Health Canada laid charges against him."

"Why?" Leon and I ask together.

"They wanted to discredit him so the truth wouldn't get out."

"They?"

"The Alberta government, the oil companies … I don't know for sure. But I do know that oil makes people rich. And people like us … we're in their way."

"What happened to him?" I ask.

"They laid charges — tried to take his medical licence away. He fought it. Had one hell of a time. But he won. Took three years out of his life, though. Me? I'd have gone back to Ireland where he came from, but not John. He's still in Alberta. Still working with First Nations. Still flying in and out."

"He stepped up to the plate, that's for sure," Leon says.

That's an understatement.

CHAPTER EIGHTEEN

I can't stop thinking about my dream of flying like a hawk. It refuses to fade the way dreams generally do. Leon says I have a vivid imagination and that I should make movies for a living, or even write books. My grandfather says it was more than a dream; it was a vision. The more I go over it, the more I think that he might be right. The hawk gave me *his* vision, allowing me to see the earth through *his* eyes, and with *his* wisdom. He showed me the destruction. He even showed me Frank's role in it. And he showed me that the earth itself needs help. But I don't know what I'm supposed to do. Even if I was healthy, what could I do? Alone?

I ask my grandfather about this, and he tells me that when the time is right, I'll know what to do.

Leon is sleeping, so my grandfather and I talk softly. "Before the dream," I say, "I always believed Frank when he said that the industry was good for us, and for all of Canada, but now I'm seeing another side."

"I believed him too! I trusted him because he was my son. When he talked about the oil sands, I thought he meant the place we went to years ago to collect bitumen to use as waterproofing for the old canoes. I still remember it. The ground sank a little underfoot and bitumen oozed out. We left footprints, but they didn't stay for long — the earth slowly crept back to where it was before. It was like you'd never been there. I thought *that* was where Frank worked. I thought *that*'s what he was doing to Mother Earth. I thought she'd recover, as she always had, and that the upcoming generations would still be able to go there and gather bitumen. I didn't understand the scale of it, how much forest and muskeg they were destroying, how much water they were taking from the river, how much pollution they were making. But *he* knew."

Strangely, I find myself sticking up for Frank, parroting the things I've heard him say. "We're still a long way from using wind or solar. Oil is the only way right now to keep cars on the road, to keep the country moving. Anyway, the land will be reclaimed in the end."

"Throwing toxic tailings in a pit and planting spruce trees over the top isn't ever going to replace boreal forest and the life that depends on it. And as for the muskeg — they'll never be able to bring it back."

I grasp at another of Frank's straws. "They're putting money into the communities to make life better for everyone."

My grandfather grunts. "They get us sick then pay for a nice place so we can die in comfort."

"The bottom line is this," I say, hanging on to Frank's side of the fence by my fingernails, "get people to stop using so much oil, get them to build cars and planes that run on something else, get them to stop buying things that are made from plastic … then the problem goes away."

"You sound just like your father," he says, disappointment tingeing his voice. "You're putting the responsibility onto someone else. Destroying Mother Earth goes against everything that our ancestors lived for. I know it. And you know it too, in your heart. But the problem is that everyone's become accustomed to the *things* that money can buy. That goes for Frank, *and* it goes for you! So you deny what's happening to our land and water and air. You deny what's happening to all living things here. But tell me, Hawk, can money buy life?"

His voice trembles, and I know he's close to tears. I hear the silent question held in his heart. "Can money buy *your* life, Hawk?"

He sniffs, then continues. "When all the birds have fallen from the air, when the animals have vanished from the land, when fish no longer swim in the rivers — they'll be gone forever. We'll never be able to buy them back or recreate them. What good is a new truck then?"

"Gramps has a good point," Leon says sleepily.

My heart knows it's true.

CHAPTER NINETEEN

Winter loosens her grip on the frozen north. Once again, millions of birds from across the Americas fly north, the urge to mate directing them back to their breeding grounds.

It takes White Chest a mere fourteen days to migrate the three thousand miles to Northern Alberta, instinct guiding him to the old nesting site where the man-machines attacked his family and killed his off-spring. He perches close by, on one of the few trees that remain along the edge of the river. And there he waits for Three Talons.

Eventually he hears her voice. She circles over-head, calling for him to join her. He needs little encouragement. On outstretched wings the pair fly higher until they are well above the dust that swirls from the bare land. At first they wheel aimlessly, but then Three Talons makes a decision. She heads toward the distant horizon, where deep green forest touches clear blue sky. But the secluded destination she hopes to find is always just beyond her reach. The wilderness is no longer wild. Broad, straight tracks cut through ancient boreal forest. Sticky resin oozes from wounded pines, the scent overpowered by the odour of man and his machines. Close to exhaustion, the birds fly on. The responsibility of raising the next generation weighs heavy on their wings.

The nurse hands me a letter. It's from Gemma.

> *Hey Adam:*
>
> *I can't remember the last time I wrote a letter — on paper I mean, with a pen! Probably I was about seven. I had to write to my Gran. She sent me a dress for my birthday. I didn't like it. Even back then I hated to wear dresses. But Mom said I had to thank her for it anyway — and tell her that I loved it.*
>
> *I'm rambling because I don't know how to start saying what I need to say. So I guess I just have to say it. I haven't been a good friend to you. I know that. Looking back, it was obvious you weren't well. For a few months you hadn't been your best. I ran alongside you over the winter, and I slowed down so you could keep up.*

You what? Thanks for hitting me with that now.

If I'd told you that you looked like crap, instead of trying not to hurt your feelings, would you have got help sooner? Would you be this sick now? My mom says it wouldn't have made any difference, but all the same I feel bad.

<u>You</u> feel bad!

I don't like feeling like this … guilty. So I hope you'll forgive me.

<u>You</u> expect <u>me</u> to make you feel better?

Did you hear what went down at the Regionals? Allan Bidall won the gold.

Shoot! I'm so much faster than him. I <u>was</u> so much faster than him.

I came in second, but I was the first <u>girl</u> to cross the line, so I won the girls' gold. It was awesome. A real high. Even got to stand on a podium for the ceremony. Never had such an incredible feeling.

Rub my nose in it, why don't you?

The running club has a new member. Eric. We've been hanging out after training.

We went to the movies.

Crap! Gemma has replaced me! That's okay. Eric is welcome to her. I don't give a damn.

> *Guess I shouldn't be telling you any of this since you're stuck in the hospital, but what else can I tell you? It's hard to know what to say. If this was a text, I'd delete it and start over, but this is freakin' paper and pen! My hand's already cramping, so there's no way I'm starting over.*
>
> *So — short story — I'm really sorry you're sick. Hope you get better soon. Now I have to go and buy one of those things called postage stamps. Unreal!*
> *Love,*
> *Gemma*

Tears well in my eyes, and I bury my head in the pillow.

"You wanna talk?" Leon says when I come up for air.

I thrust the letter toward him.

"Is it from Chrissie?" he asks.

"No, it's from my best friend."

Leon reads in silence. When he gets to the end, he doesn't look up. Instead he folds the letter neatly along its original lines and smooths the paper.

"Melissa dumped me," he blurts out.

"What? When?" I ask in total bewilderment.

"Twenty-four days ago."

"But you said …"

"I know."

"I'm sorry, Leon," I whisper. I don't know what else to say.

CHAPTER TWENTY

The wolves lope down the broad man-track. White Chest and Three Talons swoop low over their backs. The young ones are almost fully grown, but they play as they run, bumping into one another, making a grab for the scruff of a neck, or a tail. The adults, however, are single-minded. They are hunting. With heads low to the ground, muscles rippling under sleek coats, and tongues lolling from open mouths, they sniff the trail as they run. They are tracking their favourite prey.

The pair of fish hawks let the warm air carry them upward. From high in the sky, they see the mother caribou that the wolves can only smell. Weak wolf-eyes have not yet spotted her in the dappled light under the trees, although she *is well aware of them. Alert, she stands over her newborn calf.*

Head raised.

Nostrils twitching.

Every muscle in her body tense.

The wolves follow the strengthening scent, closing in.

The birds settle on a tree limb to watch and wait.

I'm waiting for Leon to come back. Not that he's gone anywhere, at least not physically. But he's so depressed these days that it's like he's not here. I've tried to lift his spirits — so has Gramps — but it doesn't help much. Leon won't talk about the break-up. He won't talk about anything. It hits me that although Leon got the news weeks ago, he hadn't accepted it until he blurted out the confession to me. He'd been living in denial. Now he's facing reality. I can relate. Reality is something we all have to grapple with in this place.

My reality is that although I'm supposed to be getting better, it's not happening. I'd been looking forward to going home for a while. But that's not happening either.

Slowly and carefully, the mother caribou picks her way toward the wolves, away from her calf, who remains motionless in a bed of tall grass. The top prong of her antlers catches a pine branch.

She stops dead. The wolves stop dead too, their eyes searching for movement that would give her away.

Springing from her hiding place, she bounds onto the track and gallops flat-out. The wolves see her for the first time, a blur of speed and aroma. They leap after her but are slower off the mark. With barely a swing of her head, she sees that the wolves are lagging. She slows, letting them gain ground. And then she swerves, charging into the undergrowth, leaping over fallen trees and ducking under branches.

The wolves follow but soon lose her in the dense undergrowth. The caribou circles back to the start of the chase, to the patch of grass flattened by the slight weight of her calf.

He's not there.

The smell of blood fills the air.

The birds sense the caribou's panic. Instinct tells her to survive — to bolt to safety. But the scent of her offspring still clings to the earth, and her legs will not carry her away.

She pushes her nose through the trampled grass, inhaling every last trace of him. Then she throws her head back and bellows. Ears pricked, she waits to catch his reply.

There is none.

White Chest circles effortlessly on outstretched wings. From on high, he sees the other caribou in her small family herd. They moved on while she was calving, but each time she tries to rejoin them, her nose follows the scent of her calf in the opposite direction — along the trail where wolf pads have broken the foliage and where their odour is still strong.

She's indecisive. Alone. Vulnerable.

She thrusts her antlers angrily at the enemy.

But there are no wolves to fight.

And no calf to fight for.
She stays a while, moaning. Eventually she walks
away.

CHAPTER TWENTY-ONE

The rising air carries White Chest and Three Talons high above the wolves and the caribou. Their powerful eyes scan the landscape for that elusive place of wilderness and solitude. Beneath their wings, a helicopter swoops after the wolves. A man leans out of the side.

The wolf pack is strung out, the old ones straggling.

Pop! Pop! Pop!

Wolves fall, some dropping like stones, others staggering.

Only one escapes. Wounded, he crawls into the bush.

Each day, I feel worse than the day before.

I'm supposed to be getting better.

In my heart I know I'm not.

White Chest and Three Talons use the last of their strength to reach the great lake where man-machines

do not go. They find a dying spruce already topped with the remains of an abandoned osprey nest. Taller than the surrounding trees, it offers easy access for their large wings and provides an unmatched view of the land-scape. And there, in the solitude, the courtship ritual finally begins. No one sees White Chest dance in the sky. No one is around to be awed by the strength that it takes for him to hover like a hummingbird or swoop like a swallow or soar like an eagle. White Chest goes through these difficult manoeuvres for one pair of eyes alone, those of Three Talons, his lifelong mate. Despite their commitment to each other, and despite his fatigue, he still has to impress her each spring. Three Talons screams her encouragement every time he swoops toward her, and in due course she accepts his gift of fish.

Leon is gone!

For the longest time he's been in the bed next to me, and even though big chunks of time have flown by, leaving me confused about where they went, Leon has always been there when I've opened my eyes. Until I open my eyes and he *isn't* there. Another kid is in his bed. I panic.

"Who are you?" I demand.

The boy turns away from me without replying. He has hair.

There's a note on my table: *Been discharged. Gone home. Leon.*

I hadn't thought that I could sink any lower, but this takes me to a whole other level.

My running coach often talked about "hitting the wall." It's that moment when you've been running a long distance and suddenly you feel like you're trying to drag an elephant behind you. Muscle coordination flies out the window. You can't even put one foot in front of the other. I feel like that now. I've hit the wall. I've run out of strength. I've run out of energy. I've run out of enthusiasm and drive. I've run out of everything. Empty! That's how I am, and no matter how long I sleep, or how many days I lounge around doing nothing, I can't get my energy back. I'm tired, in body and spirit.

I want to quit.

CHAPTER TWENTY-TWO

The birds get down to remodelling the old nest. Even a length of fishing net makes its way into the framework of the nest. Three Talons lays two eggs, but one has a shell that is soft to the touch. Three Talons senses its fragility and responds with exceptional tenderness, but it doesn't take long for it to break under her weight. The developing embryo spills out and dies.

One egg remains.

My grandfather comes and goes, as does my mother.

I can't keep track of their movements any more than I can keep track of the time.

I want to go home.

I can't.

A month later, a star-shaped crack appears on the shell of the remaining egg. Three Talons cocks her head from side to side, listening to the cheeps from inside.

Soon the chick emerges, its white down streaked with brown. Totally helpless, all it can do is open its beak and beg to be fed. White Chest brings fish to the nest, and Three Talons rips off tiny morsels, placing them directly into the chick's gaping mouth.

Something has gone wrong with time — or my ability to measure it. Sometimes I feel as if I've been here about three weeks, but then it's as if I've spent my whole life here. Weird.

The sun stays above the horizon for eighteen hours each day, giving White Chest and Three Talons plenty of time to hunt. The chick devours all of the food that they bring, changing quickly into a long-legged youngster whose appetite grows along with her body. Three Talons leaves the nest for the first time in weeks, joining her mate in the search for fish. They are taking a chance. An eagle could steal the youngster away. But the pair of hawks have not seen an eagle all summer, and food is now the priority. They can no longer be fussy about the type of fish they bring home, about the taste, or the smell. The demanding chick eats everything she is offered and instantly cheeps for more.

The youngster's feathers start to poke through the baby fluff, making her look like a porcupine, but soon she is sleek and fully fledged. Already the size of her father, and with the same brown necklace as her mother, she appears to be an adult. But her eyes are still the brilliant red of a juvenile, and she still demands to be fed. Three Talons and White Chest respond to her angry screams by bringing more fish.

Life is passing.
My life.
Passing.

CHAPTER TWENTY-THREE

The long days of the warm Alberta summer are fading. White Chest and Three Talons are driven to hurry their offspring along, their innate wisdom telling them that soon they must leave. Staying too long in Alberta is a death sentence; no osprey can survive the plummeting temperatures and frozen lakes of Canada's north.

They perch on a nearby tree limb, a fish draped at their feet. The youngster in the nest is hungry, and food is just a short distance away. She walks in circles, pecking at her feet. Then she stands on the rim of the nest, flaps her wings, and screams. Soon her developing wings are able to lift her a few inches into the air. But something holds her back. She screams in fury.

White Chest and Three Talons do not give in to her demands. They know she must be able to fly and to catch fish before the start of the long migration. They encourage her with their voices and tempt her with food, all the while remaining alert for any sign of danger. They sense none in this peaceful place. The biggest danger is the approaching winter.

Angela quit her job because she wants to be with me. I think this happened months ago, but then again, it could have been just last week. Today she's taking me to visit Leon. He's just been readmitted and is in a private room. She helps me from my bed to the wheelchair and pushes me along the corridor. When I first arrived here I was able to pop the occasional wheelie. Now I can't even push myself along.

It's been a long time since I saw Leon. I've missed him. I want to tell him my latest news: that the chemotherapy isn't working and that I'm on a bone marrow transplant list. I want to know what he thinks about the fact that I might get bone marrow from a total stranger, living or dead. I think it's creepy.

I rehearse the monologue in my mind as we trundle down the corridor, but when I get to the part about my grandfather being too old to be tested as my bone marrow donor, my eyes start to water. I know that I'll never get the words out without falling apart. It'll be game over. I'm okay venting anger, spewing out venom like an angry snake. I'm not so good with that gut-wrenching, turning inside-out of myself that seems to sneak up on me the moment my eyes start welling up.

Angela knocks on the open door and pushes me in. Leon's mother looks up. She's been crying,

I can tell. Her face is flushed, and she's kneading a wad of tissues in her hand. I get a sinking feeling.

"I was going to get coffee," Angela says to her. "Would you like to join me? That way the boys can catch up."

Leon nods his approval.

Angela places her arm over the other woman's shoulder as they walk away. It's unusual for her, since she's not exactly a touchy-feely person. I suddenly see how much my cancer is changing my mother. It isn't just my disease; it belongs to my family too.

"What's up?" I say to Leon the second they leave the room. It's a loaded question. I know it. He knows it.

"They're gonna amputate my leg tomorrow."

My heart leaps to my throat, and a wave of nausea hits me. I don't know what to say. I almost deny it. I almost blurt out the same stupid things that people said about my leukemia — things like, you're kidding me or are you sure? But I stay silent. I have no words for what I feel. Tears flood my eyes and soon both of us are bawling. I want to hug him, but I'm too weak to get out of the chair. He gets out of bed. The two legs that stick out from under his gown both look fine to me. He leans over and hugs me.

Our mothers come back to find us puffy-eyed, making light of the whole situation. But my heart is so heavy, I feel as if I weigh a ton. Angela and I return to my ward in silence. As we roll along the corridor, I think back to when I first got sick. I had thought I was tired then, but now I don't even have the strength to wheel myself. And both Leon and I are facing such a terrifying future — or no future at all.

I drag myself back into bed, hoping to hide in sleep, but I keep thinking about Leon's leg, and it makes me feel sick.

CHAPTER TWENTY-FOUR

Hunger eventually drives the young fish hawk toward her parents and the smell of fish. Her wings beat wildly, but something is tangled around her talons, holding her captive to the nest. On and on she flies, going nowhere, until exhaustion overcomes her. Her wings falter, and she begins to fall from the sky.

Until she is jerked to a stop.

She dangles from the nest by one leg, held fast by fishing net wrapped tightly around her talons. She flaps, trying to reach the safety of the rim, the talons of her free leg clutching wildly at air. But it's futile.

Eventually she runs out of strength and remains still.

Three Talons brings a fish and drapes it over the edge of the nest, but the young bird is hanging head down and doesn't have the strength to pull herself up. White Chest uses all his skill as a flyer to briefly hover alongside the ensnared bird, trying to feed pieces of fish into her beak. There is nothing else he can do.

Icy fingers start to creep down from the Arctic, threatening to hold Alberta in a frozen grasp. White Chest and Three Talons go their separate ways, flying south on different flight paths, leaving their lifeless youngster swinging in the cold wind.

I have no eyelashes. Nothing to hold back the tears.

I don't care if Angela sees me crying. I don't care if the whole world sees. Anyway, Angela is crying too. Leon's leg is all either of us can think of. Eventually she decides we should distract ourselves by watching TV in the lounge. A bull goes head-to-head with a Spanish bullfighter. They dance around each other, circling, challenging, locking eyes, waiting for that moment when one or other makes the killing charge. It's not very uplifting. We switch to the Comedy Channel, but even though the jokes are probably really funny, neither of us gets them. She wheels me back to my room and we keep on crying.

That night, in a dream, the bull from the TV comes to me, snorting hot, angry breath down my neck. Even in the dream I know that he's more than a bull. He's cancer! And I'm a skinny little matador, puny and weak, shrinking away from him, cowering against the walls of the bullring. Leon is with me. He's a matador too, slumped on the ground, legless. I want to protect him, but I can't even protect myself.

The bull paws the ground, kicking up the dust with his hooves. I scream at him, telling him he's a bully and that it's not a fair fight because Leon doesn't have any legs — I *know* that Leon still has *one* leg, but in my dream he's legless. The bull doesn't care either way. I try reasoning with him, explaining that if he kills us, *he* dies too, because a dead human equals dead cancer! He backs off.

When a cheery nurse wakes me up in the morning, I'm exhausted, as if I haven't slept for weeks. But as soon as Leon comes into my mind, it's like I've stuck a fork in an electrical outlet. A shock goes right through me. I keep checking the time, imagining Leon being wheeled toward the operating room. I want to be there, to support him in some small way, but I want to run and hide too. So it's a good thing the choice isn't mine to make.

In my mind, Leon goes through the double doors to the operating room. Just as they close behind him, my oncologist drops by. He has good news. Frank's bone marrow is an unbelievable ten out of ten match with mine! That's as good as it gets, as if we're identical twins. How can that be? I don't even like him, yet he and I have identical parts! And he has the ability to save my life. I was surprised that he'd even volunteered to be tested, and now that we know he's a perfect match, I wonder if he'll want to go through with the painful procedure of extracting marrow from his hip bones. It's one thing to be tested but another thing to do it!

The oncologist leaves, and Leon surges back into my mind, along with a mouthful of acid that makes my throat burn. The phone rings. It's Frank. He tells me how pleased he is to be a match, and that he has no reservations about being my donor, that it's his way of finally being able to do the right thing for me, to start making amends for the past. At the beginning of my leukemia journey I might have told him that I didn't want his marrow. Something deep inside of me would have wanted to deprive him of the satisfaction of saving my life. But that would be stupid, since a transplant is my best chance of survival. Anyway, the urge to hurt him is fading.

"I know I made a big mistake, leaving you behind when I left Chip," he confesses.

There's a pause on the phone line and I can hear him catch his breath, refusing to exhale. I wonder how long he can go without breathing. I know that he's holding more than his breath. He's holding his emotions, hanging on to them tight so they don't spill over. I know this because I used to do the same thing. I still do some days, but I'm becoming more familiar with emotion. My counsellor says it's better to let it out appropriately, instead of stuffing it down where it feeds the sickness inside me. Appropriately? What's with that? Like I schedule a time to be angry? And another time to be scared. Frank is so much older than me. How come he hasn't learned any of this yet? Maybe it's because he's never had cancer.

On the other end of the phone line, a breath exhales slowly.

"I wish I'd stayed and raised you, instead of going to McMurray. I know it's created a wedge between us. All I can say is that it wasn't your fault. It was mine. I hope that one day you'll forgive me."

I don't know if I'll live long enough to understand how my father could have abandoned me, but at the moment I don't feel angry toward him. I feel kind of soft and tender, like I do toward the cat that lives next door to us back in McMurray. There's something about that cat that makes me forgive the fact that he ate a bird right in front of me. Maybe I'm beginning to forgive Frank.

When he hangs up, hope surges into my heart, hope that Frank's bone marrow will defeat my cancer once and for all. But then Leon comes back into my mind, and I feel a twinge of guilt for thinking about myself. I check the time. The surgeon should be doing it right now — sawing through Leon's leg. I grab a kidney bowl from the side table and heave.

CHAPTER TWENTY-FIVE

They are killing the cancerous stem cells in my own bone marrow. *Again!* This time to prepare me for the bone marrow transplant. I try to visualize winning the battle that rages inside me, the way my counsellor suggests. But I struggle with it. Instead, I fight the cancer bull when he comes to me in my dreams, toxic fumes seeping from his nostrils. Night after night, I'm a skinny, whimpering matador, trying to stand tall, trying to be brave. But no matter how hard I try, I end up cringing against the walls of the bullring.

But then one night, something shifts. I enter the ring again, but this time *I'm* the bull. I step out of the shadows into the centre of the bullring, my sleek, black coat glistening in the sunlight. I paw at the dry earth, feeling powerful, looking for the matador to destroy. I see him in the shadows, pressed tightly against the wall, curled into a ball. It's Leon. I don't want to kill Leon. I move closer and get a shock. It's not Leon. It's me! I'm the matador. But I'm also the bull. I don't get it. I look down at my hooves, then back to the matador. I'm still *here*. I'm still *there*. *What the hell!*

When I wake up, an echo of the dream is still with me. I try to make sense of it. Suddenly, I realize what it means. I want to tell Leon, but he's in a surgical ward in a different part of the hospital, and my immune system is shot, so I'm not allowed visitors apart from immediate family who are gowned and masked. I send him a text.

> 6.01 a.m.
> I'm the bull … and the matador!

What????

> 6.03 a.m.
> In the dream.

The bullfighting dream?

> Yes. Cancer isn't some outside force attacking us. Cancer is us! Cancer is our own body cells gone crazy. We're fighting ourselves!

Then how do we win?

> I don't know.

6.08 a.m.
Are u wearing black spandex

> Huh?!

With sparkles?

> What?!

134

Matador costume?
Little vest?
Red cape?

> 6.10 a.m.
> Omg, Leon. No way!

Hey cuz …
I'd wear those leotards any
day …
if I had the choice …

> I lied, Leon! I WAS wearing
> spandex in the dream!

6.11 a.m.
Shut up!!!!!!!!!!
With sparkles down the side?

I can hear Leon's voice in the text message. It makes me smile as I reply …

> 6.12 a.m.
> Oh yeah! ☺

A few days later, I'm strapped on a gurney and wheeled out of the hospital into an ambulance. I want to gulp down fresh air before the ambulance door closes, but they won't let me take off my mask because I have no immunity and I might inhale a germ! I'm driven farther south, farther away from home, right on down to Calgary. Several nauseating hours later, I'm wheeled into the Bone Marrow Transplant Unit.

It's scary. The staff are gowned — not in disgusting hospital gowns like mine that tie down the back and leave me flashing my butt. Their gowns are like space suits, complete with booties, gloves, face masks and shower caps! All you can see of them are eyes. They even communicate in space talk, counting backward to lift off! I enter on Day Ten. Day Zero is Transplant Day.

I'm put in a positive-pressure room where only highly purified air is allowed in. Double doors are kept locked so that I can't get out, and hopefully germs can't get in. Because that's the whole point. In preparation for the infusion of precious new stem cells from my father's bone marrow, they are going to totally irradiate my entire body until every single one of my own stem cells is dead. My entire immune system will be wiped out!

Counting down.

Sinking further into hell: an underworld of diarrhea and vomiting.

I feel as if my guts have been spewed out from both ends. My rear end is plastered in antiseptic waterproofing cream, like a baby with diaper rash. And despite mouthwashes and antibiotics, my mouth is filled with cankers.

I don't mind that I'm in isolation; I don't want anyone to see me like this. But I miss my mom. And I have to stay here *after* the transplant too! My father's stem cells will need time to multiply in my bone marrow and build back my immune system. Until then, I'm at risk of infection.

Day Zero comes and goes.

I don't know how many days go by, because I'm out of it for long stretches. I don't get it. The transplant was supposed to make me feel better. That's what they said. But I feel really bad. A fireworks display is going on somewhere behind my eyes, and my head is filled with jackhammers. Monitors around me beep and peep, everything out of synch, crashing and banging like a rock band playing together for the first time. It's hard to sleep with all the ruckus going on, but I'm so tired.

I wake up to find that I'm moving, rolling along a corridor. Then I'm flying, but not like a bird. I think I'm in a plane.

Where's Angela? Why isn't she here?

Panic surges up my throat, filing my mouth like barf.

I'm alone.

It's quiet. I hear only the pulse of hospital machinery. Rhythmic and restful. *Whoosh … shhh. Woosh … shhh.* It comes and goes in gusts, like the wind that blows off the lake in summer. I wonder if this machine is keeping me alive. For the briefest moment, I feel myself slipping away. I don't fight it. *Whoosh … shhh.*

I'm a small boy being tossed into the air by my grandfather. "Again!" I squeal, "Higher!" A smile creases my grandfather's face, and his eyes light up as he tosses me higher, until I'm flying like a bird. I stretch my arms from fingertip to fingertip, and the breeze lifts me, rushing past me; pulsing and peaceful. *Whoosh … shhh.*

Everything beneath me is misty, yet I know that somewhere down there my grandfather is waiting for me to come back. But the sheer thrill of flight wipes this thought away, and I want to go on, carried by the air currents, higher and higher. Suddenly I burst out into a dazzling blue sky. *Whoosh.* Then perfect peace. *Shhhhhhhhhh.*

A fish hawk flies alongside me. I've never met this bird before. He's not the white-chested one we rescued from the tailings pond. He's more regal, like the King of the Osprey. He surges ahead, and I follow, imitating his movements, taking my flying skills to the next level. Hugging my wings to my sides, I tilt my head and dive through the air, hurtling downward. The wind rushes against me. I can barely breathe, but I'm not afraid. In the roar of the wind, I hear the voice of the hawk telling me to throw back my head and open my wings. I do as he says. I stop falling and level out. Gliding on gently angled wings, I flutter my feathers and land next to the king on his throne, on top of the highest spruce in the land.

He turns to look at me, and my own thoughts vanish, swallowed up in his incredible eyes

— gleaming like gold in the sun, fierce and piercing.

He looks down. I follow his gaze. The water of the lake beneath us is calm and clear, and I see silver fish swimming close to the surface. They're not the lively darting ones that I remember from my childhood. They move slowly and listlessly. Instantly, I know that these fish feel just like I did when the leukemia started. Exhausted. Lethargic. Heavy.

A female fish hawk magically appears next to the king. She brings images that linger on my inner eye: dead and dying chicks; eggs with shells as fragile as tissue paper. Along with these images comes the smell of rotting fish. My stomach heaves.

I look back at the King of the Osprey, hoping for an explanation, but instead his gratitude pours fast and furious into my heart. He's thanking me for saving White Chest from the tailings pond! Then he tells me that many other birds need to be helped — that his entire species is at risk — that all of nature is in danger! His proud, strong body slumps, and defeat settles on his shoulders like a heavy coat. He asks if I will help.

Whoosh. I'm back in the hospital bed.

CHAPTER TWENTY-SIX

There's plastic underneath the pillow slip. I can feel it. I can hear it rustle, but I can't move my head. Someone else is pressing on the pillow, making the plastic crackle like dry leaves. It's Frank! He leans over to kiss my cheek. Warmth floods my chest. I'm glad he's here, but I know that his presence means I'm seriously sick. A thought flashes into my mind: He's come to say a final goodbye because I'm dying!

Then another thought: I'm already dead!

He hovers over me, his hand gently stroking my forehead. He's making strange snuffling noises.

And then his tears fall quietly on my face.

I feel like crying too, but my face won't crumple, my eyes won't open, my tears won't come. All I can do is cry inside.

"I'm so sorry, son," my father says, his voice soft and trembling. "I'm so sorry that you are here like this. I wish I could trade places with you. I wish it was *me* here, and you were running your marathons just like you always did. I wish I'd been a better father. I wish —"

His sobs get heavier. My pillow rustles again as his weight shifts. And then he's walking away.

I call out for him in my head, asking him to come back, but he doesn't hear me.

He's gone.

My mother, my father, my grandfather. They're all here now. They think I'm in a coma! I've heard them say it. But I'm here. I can't force my eyes open to see them. I can't wiggle a finger. I can't make a sound!

They ask, "What went wrong? Why did this happen? Why is he like this? When will he get better? *Will* he get better?" But nobody gives them answers, and they're worried — I can tell.

I'm not worried.

I'm peaceful in this place, coming and going like waves rolling up the beach; I'm here and then I'm gone. But even when I'm here, no one can tell. They kiss my cheek or pat my hand then talk among themselves. Frank and my grandfather sit on opposite sides of my bed, each with a hand resting on mine, talking to each other.

"Dad, I'm sorry I left Adam with you. I'm sorry I didn't take care of my own son."

"Don't be sorry on my account," my grandfather says hastily. "Hawk was the best gift you ever gave me."

But my father plows on as if he really needs to get this off his chest. "I was irresponsible, leaving him behind for all those years."

"Hawk gave me a reason to get up in the morning. He made me feel young again. And useful. I became his *father*, not his grandfather. He was my second chance. Your mother and I messed up the first time. We weren't good parents to you. We had our problems, going way back before you were born. Anyway, what I'm trying to say is this … Hawk was my new beginning. So don't feel bad about leaving him with me. If you want to feel bad about something, then feel bad about taking him away. When you sent that ticket, when I put him on that plane … you broke my heart."

"I'm sorry," Frank mumbles.

I hear the familiar scrape of a chair on the floor and listen to my father's footsteps as they trail off down the corridor.

My grandfather stays, holding my hand.

"That boy is always running away," he mumbles.

At first I think he means me. Then I realize he means my father.

CHAPTER TWENTY-SEVEN

Voices come and go in waves. Or is it me who comes and goes in waves? It's hard to figure out.

"Hey, Adam."

It's a voice I know, but I can't quite place it.

"How are you?" The voice is soft and caring. It's Gemma! Behind closed lids, I see her, strands of black hair escaping from her ponytail, tanned skin, eyes … er … green, I think. Chrissie's are blue, I know that for sure. Pale blue with darker flecks.

"Can he hear me?" Gemma asks.

Angela replies. "We don't know, but we talk to him as if he can."

I try to move, to say that I'm awake, but my limbs don't respond any more than my voice does. And there is still darkness in my eyes.

The chair at the side of my bed moves. "Here, sit down," Angela suggests. "I could use a short break."

"I can't stay," Gemma says.

I hear anxiety in her voice. She's uncomfortable with the reality of seeing me like this, and she wants to get back to the world where normal people live, where healthy people live. I don't blame her. I'm dead weight.

"If you could stay just *five* minutes," Angela says, "it would be a big help to me. I don't like to leave him alone, you see, and I really need to make a phone call."

"Okay," Gemma replies.

My mother has manipulated her into staying, and that makes me feel bad for Gemma. She sits at my bedside. She fidgets. She sighs.

"I don't know what to say," she says.

In my head I say, *That's a first.*

But it doesn't take her long to find a voice. "All of this makes everything in my life seem so trivial. Like what can I tell you? Even assuming you can hear me! How could you possibly be interested in my life and in what I'm doing … when you're here like this? I mean, how petty is it that I came to Edmonton this weekend to go shopping at Canada's biggest mall?

I'm in Edmonton? That's news to me. Last time I checked I was in Calgary.

"Tomorrow we're going to the Water Park and the roller coasters."

I hear the faint sounds of fidgeting.

"I already bought a pair of running shorts," she says.

I want to know what colour they are.

It's as if she reads my mind. "They're purple. And *so* pretty. That breathable fabric, you know. And I got a pair of super lightweight runners too. They're awesome, like having feathers on your feet. I should be able to do some major mileage with them. And the best part is they're made from recycled material. Things like that are important, right?"

Again the silence. Her breathing falls into rhythm with the soft sounds of my machinery. I feel sure that she's counting down the seconds until my mother returns and lets her off the hook. I wish I could tell her that it's okay for her to leave, that she doesn't have to stay here, that she should get back to the stores and the roller coasters and the wave pool, and do all the things that she came to Edmonton to do.

But then she leans in close. I breathe her smell. It's clean and soapy. She strokes the back of my hand with her soft fingers. I sense that she feels sorry for me, like I'm a dog that got hit by a car. She clasps my hand in both of hers, and suddenly my fingers are pressed against her cheek.

"I really, really hope you get better," she whispers. There's a quiver in her voice, and I know she's close to tears.

Angela comes back into the room, and Gemma drops my hand as if she's embarrassed, like we've been caught doing something wrong.

"I'll come back another time," she says.

CHAPTER TWENTY-EIGHT

Blood pounds through my head.

Whoosh … hhhh.

Whoosh … hhhh.

I'm drifting. But when I'm here, Frank and my grandfather are here too — arguing.

"The river has *always* had oil in it," Frank says. "The whole damn riverbed is on oil sand. Rain trickles through it to get to the river. There's no more oil in the water now than there was before the industry came up here."

"The river may have always had oil it, but the fish were never sick and the people were never sick."

Whoosh … hhhh.

Whoosh … hhhh.

It sounds like waves lapping against the shore. It makes me think of the beach in front of my grandfather's cabin. I want to go there, but I'm stuck here, immobile.

In my mind, I hold my arms out, imagining them stretched from fingertip to fingertip, waiting for the whoosh to lift me skyward.

But I don't fly away. I'm still here.

"And I don't see why you get so worked up about the delta," Frank says. "The oil industry will never mine there."

"They don't need to *mine* the delta to destroy it," my grandfather replies. "All they have to do is reduce the water that passes through it. And they're doing that already. How can it be a delta if it dries up? And what happens to all the life there?"

"The delta is a World Heritage site," my father explains. "They'll look after it."

My grandfather's voice is angry. "Sometimes, Frank, I think you're blind."

And then *Whoosh*.

I'm flying — riding the thermals above Lake Athabasca, the King of the Osprey at my side. I'm thrilled to see him again, but he brings heaviness. I know that he's going to lay something on my heart. I tell him, respectfully, that although I'd love to help him, I've got so many problems of my own, and so many limitations, the main one being that it seems I might be dying! He doesn't argue with me. Instead, he invites me to follow him. There's nothing I would rather do.

We soar over a maze of meandering rivers, wriggling streams, tiny ponds, and bigger lakes, all glinting and gleaming and sparkling under a bright blue sky. Even the damp muskeg glistens like diamonds in the afternoon sun. From way down below me, I hear my grandfather's voice. "The *world* recognizes the delta as an important place, yet people here turn a blind eye. They are dazzled by dollars, not Creation!"

We circle higher, yet still the delta expands beneath my wings like an enormous cluster of jewels. It's so beautiful that I feel like crying! My grandfather's words float up to me. "Nothing is too big or too beautiful for man to destroy."

The King of the Osprey tells me to look south toward the horizon, to where a band of cloud hangs above the desolate land. At first I don't understand what he wants me to see. He tells me to look harder. It's only then that I see that the band of cloud is not normal cloud. It comes from the smoking chimneys.

I get a sinking feeling and start to tumble. Accelerating. Falling from the sky like a stone. Diving through the hospital roof as if it's thin air. For a fraction of a second, I see my mother praying. Then I see myself lying in bed, my father and my grandfather sitting at my side. I swoop back into my body and am once again a prisoner.

Immobile.

Silent.

CHAPTER TWENTY-NINE

I'm trapped in my own body. Nothing works except for my hearing. I tune into footsteps in the corridor, noticing the difference between the confident steps of the doctors, the weary walk of nurses, and the worry of fearful parents who rush past my room to see their own children.

But then I hear my own feet, pounding the trail. I'm running! I'd rather be flying, but it seems I get no choice in things these days. I'm on a trail. It's not the game trail packed down by generations of animals moving in single file — not the woodland trail untouched by the summer sun. Instead, it's a broad dirt road torn through the forest.

A helicopter swoops over my head, the rotor blades furiously slicing the air, flattening the bush: *Whup-whup-whup-whup. Whup-whup-whup-whup.* I duck low and run faster, but the helicopter hovers close, whipping dust into my face and peppering my bare arms with grains of sand. It stings.

Suddenly I'm surrounded by wolves. They are panting hard, fangs gleaming. But they aren't after me. They're trying to outrun the chopper that ruffles their fur and hurls grit into their eyes.

Pop! Pop! Pop!

My heart almost leaps out of my chest, panic giving me an incredible burst of speed to escape the gunfire. Then I remember the cannons at the tailings pond, and I breathe a sigh of relief: the pops are just noise to frighten away the birds. We're safe.

Pop! Pop!

This time louder. I look up and I'm horrified. Flashes of gunfire come from the silver helicopter. The wolves ahead of me are falling, some dropping like stones, others staggering, yowling.

The wolf alongside me yelps and stumbles. He struggles to stay on his feet and keep running, but he can't do it.

He falls.

I stop too, unable to leave him.

He crawls toward me, dragging himself on his belly, his amber eyes imploring me to save not just him, but his kind.

I don't know what to do, but I know that I'm the only help he has. I use all of my strength to drag him off the track and into the bush.

The helicopter makes a tight turn and swoops low over us. I catch glimpses of it through the branches, patrolling the sky like a prehistoric bird, ominous and deadly — shooting at the dying wolves until they are still and silent.

In the shelter of the trees, the wounded wolf with the amber eyes licks my hand.

Whoosh.

I'm back in the hospital, but I've brought the wounded wolf with me in my heart. I feel a tear slip down my cheek.

"Oh, my God!" my mother shouts. "He's crying."

She shakes my shoulders, roughly. "Wake up! Please! Please wake up, son." There's such desperation in her voice that I want to do it, but I can't. Not quite.

There's a lot of activity around me, a lot of questions asked, a lot of orders given. "Why's he crying? What does it mean? Is he in pain? Page the doctor! Is he conscious? If you can hear me, squeeze my hand."

I squeeze. My mother's shriek almost deafens me. Then she comes into view. She's fuzzy, but it's her! She looks beautiful, even though her face is scrunched up in an ugly cry. I want to tell her that I can see her. But I'm too tired. I'll tell her later, after I've had a nap. Angela screams at me not to go back to sleep, but I can't help myself.

CHAPTER THIRTY

A shy and shaggy wood buffalo takes tentative steps toward me until his wet nose gently touches my hand. It's a polite introduction. He's even bigger than the cancer bull. He could kill me with a toss of his horns or a swipe of his head if he wanted to, but there's nothing threatening in his body language. His eyes are soft and gentle, and I'm not afraid. I even want to wriggle my fingers into his thick brown coat, but I can't move. The buffalo seems to know this. He leans his shoulder lightly against me, allowing his fur to gently caress my skin. I feel special, like when the neighbour's cat, purring happily, rubs his head and body along my legs. Except this feeling is way more profound. I feel chosen! At the same time, I feel the weight of his burden. It's heavy. I'm expecting him to ask me to help, just as the osprey and the wolves did. It's like everyone thinks I can save them! But he doesn't ask a thing. He just wants me to know that he exists. His thoughts speak to me — quiet — comical: "I'm just saying."

I laugh at the absurdity of it.

I wake up and look around. Angela is curled up on the cot by the window. She's turned toward me, sleeping. I wonder what time it is. The blinds are open, and it's light outside, but I can't see the sky, just buildings of concrete and glass. Suddenly an orange glow hits the window and shines in my eyes. It must be dawn. I must have slept all night.

My mouth tastes gross and my throat is dry, like it's stuck together. I don't want to wake my mother, so I sit up, planning to swing my legs over the side of the bed, thinking I'll get myself a drink of water. But there's a cold metal railing. It's like I'm a little kid in my first "big" bed. Tubes snake all over the place too. That's strange, because I don't remember how they got there.

The simple effort of sitting up exhausts me. I collapse back onto the pillow. Angela stirs.

"Mom," I croak. "Water."

She leaps up in a single bound, clapping her hand over her gaping mouth and looking at me as if I've risen from the dead.

She tells God how good he is and how thankful she is, all the while touching me and crying tears of what I assume are joy.

"Water," I croak again.

She brings a glass with a straw and holds it for me but only lets me have a few sips. "Not too much to begin with. You've been out of it for weeks."

Weeks? I can't believe it. I feel like I've just woken up from an afternoon nap. Weird!

"Where's my grandfather?" I ask.

"He's gone back to McMurray."

"Where's Frank?"

"McMurray too. He had to get back to work. He stayed as long as he could. I'll phone him. He's going to be so happy." She dials the number. "Frank! I've got someone here who's asking about you."

She passes me the phone.

"Dad?"

My father tries to talk, but his words are lost in choking, bawling sounds. Tears flood my eyes too.

CHAPTER THIRTY-ONE

It's January, eighteen months since I was diagnosed. Finally, I'm back at the house in McMurray. I'm much better than I was, but I still feel as if I've been tipped upside down and every last bit of me has been drained out.

Even though my dad was a perfect match for the bone marrow transplant, my body still fought to reject his gift. I've often wondered if the problem was not my body at all but my stubborn, grudge-holding heart. But whichever it was, a few things went wrong and I ended up in a coma for three weeks.

Thanks to the steroids that help with the rejection, I'm now bloated like a half blown-up balloon. Plus I'm covered with fine black fuzz; my missing hair has grown back not only on my head but everywhere else too! I even have a unibrow! And I don't have a muscle left in my body. When I look at myself in the mirror, I see an old man who does nothing but sit on the couch all day, watching TV and drinking beer. But I don't have any beer. It's depressing. My mother keeps insisting that I should re-establish my old friendships, but I don't want anyone to see me like this. Except for Gemma. Apparently, she's seen me looking far worse, although I can't remember her visiting me in the hospital. In fact, that whole time in the coma is a total blur. I get a glimpse now and again, but apart from that ... nothing! It's so weird. I lost three weeks from my life. It's almost like they never happened.

Through the dark days of winter, Gemma drops in once or twice a week. Knowing she might come forces me to shower and put on clean clothes. Soon I'm looking forward to her visits and feeling that life just might be worth living after all. She says she can't wait for the day when the two of us will go running again. I think she's just trying to encourage me, but I want to believe her. It's hard, though, because I don't have the strength to stand up for longer than a couple of minutes, and I need a wheelchair to get around. Plus I have this bizarre numb sensation on the soles of my feet. Running seems as impossible as a trip to the moon, but I humour her anyway and find that it lifts my spirits. And I start to believe that one day I *will* run again, not in competition, but just on the trails. I have this crazy idea that if I can run and hold out my arms like wings, I'll be lifted into the sky and fly like a bird. I'm keeping *that* to myself.

My grandfather usually crashes my visits with Gemma. That's okay. In fact, it's probably for the best. I'm pretty sure she's not interested in me as anything more than a friend, but just in case, it's good to have him on hand! In no time, Gemma is calling him Gramps, just like Leon, and the two of them have totally bonded! I wonder how come my grandfather has this effect on people.

"My dad works for Suncor," she tells him. "He's in IT, a real nerd, but he's an environmentalist on the side too. He's concerned that the oil sands are contributing big-time to global warming." She laughs. "Not concerned enough to quit his job, though."

"Good jobs are hard to come by these days," my grandfather says.

"He's worried about the tailings ponds too, that they're too close to the river. He says that if the river ran the other way, if Edmonton and Calgary were downstream of the oil sands, there'd be hell to pay. But as it is …"

She pauses. I feel sure she's wondering if she should tell us what my grandfather already knows, and what I am learning fast.

I finish the thought for her. "No one gives a crap about First Nations living downstream, in places like Fort Chipewyan. No one cares."

"I care," she says.

My grandfather smiles. "Thank you, but you're in the minority."

"If people knew what was happening, they'd care," she argues. "We need to get the word out."

"How?" I ask.

"By telling stories like yours, Hawk."

I have no idea what she means.

"Your life story!" she explains. "Or rather your near-death story. People need to hear it."

"But leukemia has nothing to do with the industry. People all over the world get it."

Gemma looks at me as if I don't have a brain in my head. "You've gotta be kidding me."

"Even if we could prove that it was linked to pollution from the oil sands — why would anyone be interested? It's not like I'm famous. I'm not a movie star or a sports celebrity."

"You're young, and you're cute!"

"Cute?"

She grins at me, her green eyes flashing.

"First the book, then the movie!" my grandfather says, his face so straight that Gemma must think he's serious. I know he's kidding.

"You're both nuts."

CHAPTER THIRTY-TWO

It's only February, but the weather is warm. Not summer warm, just a few degrees above freezing, but it feels balmy compared to thirty below. It's too early for winter to be over. Angela says it might be a *chinook*. Frank says we don't get them this far north and that it's global warming. Whatever it is, they both seem happier than usual, like global warming is a good thing. I have to admit it makes life a little bit more worth living.

The snowbanks have been vanishing fast, leaving puddles of melted water that freeze into glare ice overnight. The sidewalks have been way too slippery for me to wheel around outside, but today the sun has dried the water, and I roll myself out of the garage. The wind is warm, and it feels great whipping through my growing hair.

And then I see Chrissie.

She's walking toward me. My heart knocks into my ribs, but I hang my head, hoping she won't recognize me. I don't want her to see me like this. And

I don't want her to leap over the slushy grey snow-bank and cross the street to avoid me. She doesn't.

"Adam!" she shrieks. "*Oh my god!* How are you?"

She towers over me, making me feel like a child sitting at a baby desk in kindergarten. I have to tip my head up to speak to her. It's more than embarrassing. She crouches down to my eye level. I feel even worse, like any moment she's going to get a sippy cup out of her bag and offer it to me. I wish I could fade right off the map. Then I'm looking into her eyes. Her crazy beautiful eyes! And I come rushing back.

"You wanna go grab a coffee or something?" she asks, her voice warm and bubbly. "I've got time to kill. What about you?"

My mind is officially blown. "Trust me!" I say. "I've got time to kill too."

"How about Tim Hortons?"

As much as I love Chrissie, as much as I'm prepared to slay a dragon for her, there's no way I'm wheeling up the Timmy's ramp, negotiating my way between the tables and chairs, risking someone else from my old life seeing me. "I'll pass! But you can come over to my place if you want."

"Sure!" she says.

Oh … my … god! It's a miracle!

I try to turn the chair around, moving it back and forth, cranking it as hard as I can, but the side-walk is way too narrow for me to make a U-turn. I want to appear independent and capable, but I'm messing up big-time, and frustration makes me annoyed. I keep it under wraps, though, not wanting Chrissie to see this side of me. I've got enough strikes against me without adding anger issues to the mix. So I laugh at myself instead.

"I got it!" she says, grabbing the handles and skilfully spinning me around. "These chairs can be such a pain."

"Yeah, what's with that?" *Crap! Is that all you can come up with?* "So where did you learn to handle a chair so well?"

"I volunteered at the seniors' home last year. My mom said I needed to get something like that on my resumé — for college applications, you know. I didn't like it much. But I learned a few tricks about wheelchairs."

Damn it! I'm in the same category as the old folks in the nursing home.

Angela beams from ear to ear when I roll through the garage with Chrissie in tow and walk the last few steps from the laundry room and into the kitchen. She instantly rushes around, making hot chocolate and opening cookies. Then, announcing that she has to do laundry, she leaves us alone. She's *not* out of earshot.

"Is your grandfather here?" Chrissie asks.

"Yeah. Why?"

"Since that day in your yard, when you rescued the osprey, I've been kind of hooked on them. And he knows *so* much!"

I stifle a sigh of disappointment. She came to see my grandfather, not me. I'm okay sharing "Gramps" with both Leon and Gemma, but sharing him with Chrissie — it's too much!

"I wonder if he made it, if he's still alive," Chrissie says.

"The osprey or my grandfather?" I say, my expression flat.

Chrissie giggles. It sounds wonderful. I can't help but laugh too.

She looks at me with a smile that lights up her face. "It's good to hear you laugh again," she says, reaching out to briefly touch my arm. Electricity zaps me, leaving me virtually senseless. I'm at a total loss for words, so I call for my grandfather to come downstairs.

Chrissie's in awe of him. "Osprey are cool, aren't they?" she says to *him,* not me. "I didn't even know they existed before you rescued that one from the tailings pond, but now I've found a place online where there's a webcam in a nest."

"Shut up!" I say, coming to my senses and forcing myself back into their conversation. "You can stream it live?"

"Yeah. But the nest is empty right now."

My grandfather gazes through the window at the sky. "The birds will be back in another month or two," he announces with that knack he has of knowing all things nature-related. "Then they'll lay eggs and raise chicks."

"Nice!" she says, staring at him as if he's David Suzuki, the biggest nature authority in all of Canada. "We'll be able to watch them on the computer!"

My grandfather frowns as if such a thing is beyond all possibility.

The two of them chatter on, and I'm sidelined — watching. She's jaw-droppingly beautiful. Suddenly my brain feels fuzzy, and I feel weak and wobbly, like I'm made of Jell-O. She still has that same effect on me.

Eventually, Chrissie notices! "Are you okay?"

I blink wearily.

"Hawk gets tired a lot," my grandfather says.

Chrissie looks at me confused, mouthing the word *Hawk*. She doesn't realize I've got a new identity!

Angela magically appears and shepherds her toward the door. "Let's not overdo things today, Chrissie. Hawk's still quite weak —"

Oh, Mom, no! Don't tell her that! Let her stay. There's nothing wrong with me.

"But please come back anytime you want. We'd love to see you."

I try to wave. I'm so tired, I can barely raise my hand.

I wake up with a jolt, the dream still vivid — Chrissie and me, climbing the rock wall at Mac Island — me ahead of her, holding out my hand to help her along. Then I lose my footing and hurtle downward, dragging her with me. Just as we're about to hit the ground, I wake up.

A sickening feeling settles in the pit of my stomach. If my wildest dreams ever became reality and if Chrissie ever became my girlfriend, I would just drag her down.

I look out the window to the dawning day. Snow is falling. Yesterday, when Chrissie visited, the sun was shining and spring was in the air. Now winter is back. The weather's on a roller coaster, and so am I. Yesterday, I was at the top of the loop, but now I'm at the bottom, and it wasn't a fun ride. I tell myself that Chrissie isn't interested in me anyway. She's interested in the osprey and my grandfather, not me. Then I cringe at the thought that she might be using me for her resumé. Did my mother promise to write her a reference letter? I'm crushed at the thought.

It's best to stay here at the bottom of the roller coaster loop, because if I climb even partway up to the top, I'm pretty sure I'll come crashing down again. And I don't like the falling part. I never liked real roller coasters either.

CHAPTER THIRTY-THREE

Gemma comes by with a newspaper.

"Gramps, have you seen this?" she says, pointing to a photo of a middle-aged blond woman. "She just died of bile-duct cancer. She worked at Syncrude with my dad. She was management but was out on-site by the tailings ponds — a lot."

I take all of thirty seconds to read the whole article. My grandfather takes much longer. He reads slowly and thoughtfully. Finally, he speaks.

"They tell us we get bile-duct cancer because we are First Nations — something about our Aboriginal genes — and because we smoke and drink and have diabetes and sit around too much. I wonder what excuse they'll come up with now."

Gemma's already heading to the door. "I can't stay, but I wanted you to see this. There might be more online. Check it out."

She's right, there's more online. The whistle-blowing doctor, John O'Connor, says that the woman had been fit and healthy, didn't smoke, didn't have diabetes. In fact, she did everything right, and the only connection to risk factors was the oil sands. But Alberta's chief medical officer says that there's little evidence of connections between oil sands pollution and cancer.

"Crap!" I say. "Even the doctors are on different sides of the fence!"

My grandfather sighs. "I'd trust John over the rest of them."

"Why didn't you tell me about him before?" I ask my grandfather. "He's famous!"

He shrugs. "I didn't get much chance, not with you moving away when you were young. Anyway, John didn't say anything about leukemia."

We're both so engrossed, we don't hear Frank come home.

"Adam's leukemia has nothing to do with the oil sands," he says, his tone indicating there's no room for discussion.

My grandfather stands up and faces Frank head-on. "Maybe, maybe not. But there's a lot of cancer in Chip. You can't deny that. Your mother! She died from bile-duct cancer, I'm sure of it."

"You don't know she died from bile-duct cancer," Frank exclaims. "There's nothing to *prove* it. Just hearsay, not science. No coroner's report or anything."

Rage flickers across my grandfather's face. "A coroner? In Chip? It's not exactly *CSI: Miami* up there. Before John came, it was hard to find a doctor to treat the *living*, let alone the dead."

"People hang on O'Connor's every word," Frank yells, "but he's just a family doctor, not a cancer specialist. Health Canada doubted his diagnoses. And so do I. They laid complaints against him, remember! They wouldn't have done that without good reason."

I stand up in a burst of anger that takes even me by surprise. Words shoot from my mouth like bullets from a gun, and my chair topples backward with a satisfying crash. "What's the matter with you?" I yell. "How come you believe everything they say ... and *nothing* we say? Gran died of bile-duct cancer ... your own father says so. Why don't you believe him? And I've got leukemia. Can't you see that there just *might* be a link to the industry ... to the river?"

I storm off as fast as my decrepit body can carry me, hurling one final order as I go. "And stop calling me Adam! I'm Hawk!"

I slam the bedroom door so hard that it rattles the picture frame on the wall; my certificate for placing second in the cross-country meet ... a lifetime ago. I reach up, yank it from the wall, and hurl it to the ground. It makes me feel better. I collapse on the bed and go back over the argument. I get hung up on something my grandfather said: that it's not exactly *CSI: Miami* in Fort Chipewyan. I imagine Horatio and his crew racing a powerboat up and down Lake Athabasca, churning up the water as they collect data from crime scenes. Pretty soon, my vision expands to include a new series: *CSI: Fort Chip*.

Part of me laughs, but part of me says that's exactly what we need: someone to treat Chip like a crime scene! Someone to collect data, not just from the rivers and lakes, the rain and the snow, and the air, but also from the fish, the fish-eating birds, and mammals. They need to collect data from *us*!

Frank knocks on my bedroom door. He looks sad. "At work, they told us they were always testing the air and the water. They said that everything was fine, that none of the levels were high enough to be dangerous. I believed them because they had science and statistics. I didn't understand science or statistics, but I trusted it. I trusted them. I really thought they knew what they were doing." He gives a snort that sounds a lot like my grandfather's trademark putdown. "They've always been the ones who told us what to do and how to do it. Your grandfather may be right. I'm a fool."

Without waiting for a response, he turns to leave. "Oh, and by the way, I'll call you Hawk from now on. It suits you."

Suddenly I'm not so angry with him anymore.

CHAPTER THIRTY-FOUR

There's been a change in the family, a kind of seismic shift. It's not just that my parents both call me Hawk now, or the fact that sometimes I let the words "Mom" and "Dad" slip out. And I wouldn't go as far as to say that we're suddenly a normal family, although who knows what that really looks like — probably nothing like in the movies. But at least we're not enemies anymore!

Frank and my grandfather still bicker, but it's different, it's more an airing of views, an expressing of opinions. And they are even sharing ancient memories! They are doing it right now. I'm working on a school paper, but their conversation about my father's childhood is more interesting than the battle of Queenston Heights and the War of 1812.

"When I was a kid, I spent more time bailing out that canoe than paddling it," my father says, laughing. It's a nice sound, one I'm still getting used to. "I was so happy when you gave up patching it with bitumen and bought the fibreglass one.

It never leaked. I remember helping you patch the cabin roof too."

"That old roof needed resealing every year," my grandfather says. "But then I got new shingles — and after that I had no need for bitumen, so I never made the long trip down the river again."

"I remember going with you once!" Frank exclaims.

"Did we take the canoe?"

"No. We used the boat with the outboard. It took several days. I can't imagine how long it would have taken by canoe."

"Not that much longer," my grandfather says. "I could paddle at quite a pace. I was young then and fit like you wouldn't believe. How old were you, Frank?"

"Nine or ten. We camped. We caught walleye, and we rammed green sticks right down the length of them and then stood them in the fire to cook. They were *big* suckers."

"That's exactly what I mean, son. The fish were much bigger big back then!"

My father doesn't reply. I wonder if he's remembering the super-sized fish of his childhood or thinking about the fact that my grandfather's theories about the fish might be right. In the lull, my grandfather goes off topic.

"I guess I can't blame the oil industry for wanting to make money. But the government ... they should have protected us." He snorts disdainfully. "What am I thinking? The government has never protected us. They make promises that sound fine, but they mislead us, and they break their word as soon as something better comes along."

"*Our* word is good for all time," my father says. "I remember you teaching me that when I was a boy: Our word is good for as long as the sun shines, as long as the grass grows, as long as the river runs."

"But now they're making it so the grass *doesn't* grow," my grandfather says, "and the river *doesn't* run."

Astoundingly, Frank agrees! "And sometimes the air is so thick that the sun doesn't even shine."

"You know, son, they've never cared about us, going right back to when they first came here, stealing the land and putting us into mission schools. They were always trying to get rid of us."

"You mean the residential school? You never talked about it."

"And I'm not going to start now," my grandfather says firmly. "It's best forgotten."

"Folks have been breaking the silence recently, telling their stories. They say it helps."

"It won't help me! If your mother was still alive, it might have helped her. She had it bad. Far worse than me. They broke her at that damn school. And she stayed broken her whole life. In the old days, we loved our children and raised them right. Every child was cared for. But by taking little kids away from their families —"

My grandfather's voice starts to tremble, and he pauses to regain control. "Rose was taken away when she was four. She didn't know what it was like to be loved by her own mother and father, so how could she pass that love on to you? How could she be a good parent? No one ever showed her how!"

"I thought it was *my* fault!" Frank exclaims, his voice cracking. "I thought I was unlovable!"

I look up from the computer and watch my grandfather take my big, strong father in his arms. They hold each other, their sobs muffled by the closeness. I almost choke up too.

Eventually, my grandfather speaks. "I tried to be both mother and father to you, Frank. I know I didn't do a very good job. I made lots of mistakes. I did a better job with Hawk."

"You did an excellent job with Hawk," my father says. "And I think I turned out okay, too."

"In the end," my grandfather says with a chuckle.

Oh my god! My illness has accomplished one giant thing. My father and my grandfather finally seem to like each other.

CHAPTER THIRTY-FIVE

The next time Chrissie drops by, I tell her that my grandfather is napping and that we need to be quiet so we won't disturb him. The truth is, I don't want him to know that she's here. I don't want to share her. She suggests we check the live stream from the webcam in the osprey nest to see if the birds have come back yet. We sit on the sofa side by side, her Mac balanced on our laps, my thigh so close to hers that I swear I can feel electricity jumping between us. The osprey haven't returned to the nest. It's still too early. I don't care. I'm far more interested in Chrissie than in what the osprey might be doing, but I don't want her to close the laptop and move away from me, so I suggest we look at video clips from last year's live stream. It works! Chrissie *oohs* and *aahs* at a newly hatched chick with bits of rust-coloured shell still stuck to its back. I look at the exact same chick, see its featherless wings folded neatly, and can't help but be reminded of chicken wings from Boston Pizza.

A young bird, almost the size of an adult, looks right into the camera. "Just look at those eyes!" Chrissie exclaims. "They're red."

"They'll turn yellow eventually, like the parents," I say, proud to be able to pass on a piece of information I learned from my grandfather. "Eye colour is the only way to tell a juvenile from an adult."

"Cool," she says, moving on to look at a pair of adults side by side. "Hey look! It's just like your grandfather said … the female has a brown necklace. And she's bigger. She's *so* pretty."

"Let's see how different osprey are from bald eagles," I suggest, desperate for ways to keep Chrissie sitting next to me.

An image of a stunningly good-looking bald eagle pops up on the screen. He makes the osprey look like a second-class citizen.

"He's got yellow feet! And a yellow beak!" Chrissie observes, studying the eagle. "And he's black all over, except for his head."

"Our osprey looked black all over too, until we cleaned him up, remember?"

"That's true. Even your grandfather wasn't a hundred percent sure to begin with. Do you think he'll be up from his nap soon?"

Oh my god. It's true! Chrissie only comes here to hang out with my grandfather.

I shrug nonchalantly. "Sometimes he sleeps for hours."

"Okay, maybe I'll see him next time," she says, proving my point. "I gotta go."

As she lets herself out, I realize that I need to take some lessons from my grandfather. I need to become an orni-what's-it-called … whatever the word is for being a bird lover. I could probably take some other lessons from him too.

I've been doing my exercises like crazy, looking down the tunnel to the day when I will saunter down the street with Chrissie, but the day for my follow-up appointment at the cancer clinic draws closer. It hangs over my head like an ominous black cloud that darkens my mood and my thoughts. What if the cancer is back? What if I have to go back for another round of chemotherapy?

The next time Chrissie drops by, she keeps asking me what's wrong. Finally, I tell her. She reaches for my hand and says that she's sure everything will be fine. I feel fragile. I lower my head, not wanting her to see this vulnerable side of me. She'll think I'm a wimp.

"It's okay," she says, gently lifting my chin. Our eyes meet.

Before I know what's happening, her lips are on mine, and she's kissing me! Briefly, I think that maybe being vulnerable isn't a bad thing. But then it all goes wrong. My nose gets in the way. There's even a little click as our teeth collide. Chrissie pulls away, and it's over. I feel inadequate and embarrassed. She gets weird, grabs her things, and leaves.

A few moments later, I wonder if the kiss was all in my imagination. The taste of strawberry lip gloss tells me otherwise.

CHAPTER THIRTY-SIX

My parents and my grandfather come with me to the appointment. They're all over me as we walk from the hospital parking lot. And in the waiting room they ask other people to move so that we can all sit together. I wonder why it has taken me so long to see that they are *all* in this with me.

Dr. Miller announces that I am doing really well. Angela gasps and hugs me, tears streaming down her face. Frank joins the hug, sandwiching me between them. Even *his* eyes glisten. My grandfather waits until they are done hugging me, and then he holds out his arms. I snuggle into him. I feel like a child again, wrapped in his love.

The only problem is … I've done such a great job of preparing myself for bad news that I can't totally take in good news! My parents, however, are overjoyed and insist on celebrating. We stop on the way home and buy a bottle of sparkling wine that Angela says is just like real champagne, except at a fraction of the price. "We're a single income family now," she reminds Frank when he suggests she should buy the real thing. He gets the job of opening the bottle, but he's never done it before, so it pops then froths all over the place. Mom laughs, glad that we didn't spend a hundred dollars on the bottle. She pours me half a glass, and we do the *cheers* thing, raising our glasses and toasting. It's a new experience for me. Dad makes a speech, saying how brave I've been and how proud of me he is. It makes me feel warm inside. Mom tries to say something too but chokes up and can't get it out. "Happy tears," she says between sobs, grabbing the tissue box. My grandfather watches from the sidelines.

Despite their words, I still feel a little hollow. I've learned that good news doesn't last long. Bad news is usually right around the corner. I take a swig from the glass. Bubbles froth down my nose, and I almost choke. My parents laugh, and pretty soon I'm laughing too. The liquid feels warm inside me, and soon my concerns vanish.

"I'm cancer-free!" I yell.

Gemma texts to see how the appointment went. Leon texts too. I reply to them both with a smiley face, a thumbs-up, and the words "CANCER-FREE!"

CHAPTER THIRTY-SEVEN

The failed kiss bothered me for a while, but I guess I made more of it than I needed to, because Chrissie still drops by sometimes on her way home from school. I long to kiss her — *need* to kiss her. It's like her lips are food, or maybe even air that I can't live without. But it's not happening — she's keeping her distance, and I'm starving and breathless.

School's over for the day. I mean, normal school for normal people. *My* school day was done hours ago. I wait at the window, hoping that today will be one of the days that Chrissie stops by … that today will be the day we kiss again. As I wait, I take stock of things. I'm able to walk farther each day. My appetite is better too, and I'm not stuck in depression any more. I'm a long way from rock climbing at Mac Island, but I *am* closer to hopping on a bus and heading into the City Centre. And as crazy as it seems, I've been thinking about where to take Chrissie on a date — some place where we'll be away from my grandfather, for starters. Start small, I tell myself. Catch the bus into town and go to Boston Pizza or the movies. Both these ideas seem too big to hope for, but I hope anyway. The harder part is figuring out how and when to ask her. I've been working on it, rehearsing in front of my bedroom mirror.

When she rounds the corner and comes into view, my heart flutters. *How nuts is that?* She's with a group … grade elevens, I think. As they get closer, some surge ahead, roughhousing on the sidewalk and spilling over onto the road. Chrissie lags behind, talking with a boy. He's tallish and good-looking. Athletic. Like I used to be.

When they reach my house, he walks on. I can tell by the way he looks back at her that he wants to be more than her friend, and my heart gets heavy.

Chrissie comes in. She's her normal cheerful self, and I try to hide my disappointment by doing what I usually do — laughing. But then I realize that I'm feeling more than just disappointment. I'm jealous! I'm totally pissed that another guy is going to snatch Chrissie away from me, and that I don't have a chance because — well, look at me. I might be in remission, but I'm still Cancer Boy. I laugh some more, until it's way over the top. She must think I'm borderline manic. My grandfather rescues me by making us tea, but then he won't leave us alone. He and Chrissie talk, and I'm the odd one out — again. I catch his eye and jerk my head toward the stairs. He gets the message and heads off to his bedroom.

"Hey, Chrissie," I say, grabbing my iPad and sitting on the sofa, "I've learned some really cool things about osprey. Come and see."

It works! Chrissie sits close to me. Her hair smells like vanilla, and it makes me feel light-headed. The letters on the screen merge into each other, but fortunately I know the information by heart. Rather than reciting it word for word, I take an interactive approach.

"Did you know that fish hawks are really important when it comes to monitoring environmental pollution?" *Damn!* I sound like a teacher.

"How come?" she asks.

"They're at the top of the aquatic food chain."

She makes that "So what?" expression.

"They eat fish, which eat smaller fish, which eat smaller fish. If the water has traces of chemicals in it …"

"Chrissie gasps. "They get a serving of poison in each meal!"

"Exactly! The chicks show signs of poisoning before the adults. They might be deformed or die. The eggs may have soft shells or even no shells at all."

Chrissie looks alarmed. "Then the species will die out! D'you know if that's happening to the birds around here?"

"I don't know."

"Does anyone know?"

I shrug.

"Let's try to find out," she says, taking over the iPad. I lean in close, pretending to read along with her.

"Look at this," she says, but I'm too busy enjoying her closeness to respond.

Her phone dings. She moves away to read the message and then says she has to leave. I walk her to the door, and figuring it's now or never, I launch into my *asking-her-out-on-a date* pitch.

"I'm really glad we're friends, Chrissie," I begin. "You'll never know how much you've helped me get through the last few weeks, and I was wondering if —"

She interrupts. "I'm glad we're friends too, but I've gotta go. I've got a date."

Her words stun me.

"I'll drop by tomorrow, okay?"

CHAPTER THIRTY-EIGHT

Chrissie doesn't drop by as she promised. She says she's busy with a science project. She's making excuses, I'm sure. She says she'll try to come the next day.

She doesn't.

It happens one more time.

Then no message. Nothing.

I know what it means. She's dating. She doesn't have time for me. I beat myself up for being so stupid. Chrissie was never interested in me as anything more than a friend, yet I let myself hope for more. *Stupid! Stupid! Stupid!* I'm at the bottom of the roller coaster. Again!

For days, I flip-flop, unable to decide if I should message her or not. Or phone or not. I decide to text.

Hey, just checking in. How R U? Miss you ♥

I delete and try again.

Hey, just checking in. How are things? ☺

And one more time.

Hey, just checking in. 👍

My thumb hovers over *Send*. I chicken out.

I'm reluctantly doing a circuit of the main floor, urged on by Angela, who promises cookies after I've walked. *How old am I? Five?* And then it happens. From the living room window, I see Chrissie in the distance. She's snuggled into the same tall-ish guy, his arm slung over her shoulder, her head against his chest, their footsteps synchronized as they head toward me. They cross the street — to be away from me, I'm sure. She does a little hopping step to keep up with his longer stride. And then they're moving away. Her sandy hair flows down her back like the mane of a wild horse. He doesn't stumble. He's energetic. He's alive! I'm sure his eyes are bright and his skin is flawless. He doesn't have a unibrow or a bloated face. I watch until they disappear from view. I feel like I should cry, but I don't. Tears won't come.

Chrissie had made me feel almost normal. But now I'm cancer boy again, the boy who will never find love. I was a fool for letting her back into my life, because here I am, wallowing in despair even deeper than before.

Angela is already fed up with my moans. Her words are kind, but what she means is, *get over it!* So I phone Leon. He listens in silence as I unburden myself. When I tell him about the problems I'm having with both my feet — that the radiation killed off too many nerves — he says, "At least you've got both feet."

Before I can respond, he hangs up.

I phone him back, but he doesn't pick up. I feel like a complete jerk.

I shuffle to the family room and park myself in front of the television. A commercial comes on for the oil sands. It shows children running through a grassy field, everything as green as nature made it. It doesn't match what I saw at Energyse: a scene that looked like a moonscape, and a fish hawk covered in oil.

A memory from my childhood flashes across my mind: my grandfather lifts me out of the boat and sets me down on the springy moss, his favourite place for gathering herbs for tea. The summer air hums with dragonflies, songbirds, and butterflies. In the distance, a moose stands knee-deep in the shallows, grazing on water weed, her calf stretching to browse lime-green leaves from a tamarack tree. Then, in my mind, I start to run … along an old game trail. In the distance I see my grandfather's cabin. The lake shines behind it.

I'm so wrapped up in my thoughts that at first I don't hear my grandfather join me.

"I want to go home," I tell him.

"You mean Chip?"

I nod.

He smiles. "Me too."

Down in the humid bayous of Louisiana and the warm marshes of Texas, White Chest and Three Talons are feeling the urge to head home too. The subtle lengthening of the days tugs at their wings, telling them that soon it will be time to start the long flight north to the place where they were born. Instinct drives them to fish more and eat more, thus building the strength to endure the gruelling flight home.

CHAPTER THIRTY-NINE

The idea of me returning to Fort Chipewyan with my grandfather scares my mother half to death.

"You're still weak," she protests, "still vulnerable to infection. If something goes wrong, you'll be so far away from the hospital. I can't face —"

Her words get blotted out by an upheaval of emotion. "You can't face the possibility of losing me?" I suggest.

She nods and bawls some more. I hug her, but her tears come even faster.

"The problem is," my dad tells her, "you've been so caught up in looking after Hawk all this time. It's become part of your life. It's who you are!"

My mother seems stunned at my father's insight. "I know," she blubs, "I want to baby him. I want to protect him from the world. We've all been through so much."

I want to tell my mother that she's making this all about her, but that seems a little cruel, so I stay silent.

My father is on a roll of newfound wisdom. "You have to start letting go, Angela. It's time to pick up the pieces of your old life."

My grandfather stays out of it other than to assure my parents that he's perfectly capable of looking after me and that there's a beautiful new medical centre in Chip. "No full-time doctor," he says, "but the nurses are good. And they've got Medivac. In an emergency, he'd be flown back here in no time."

After a week of uncomfortable conversations around the dinner table, Mom says I can go! She says they'll get Internet set up in the old cabin so I'll still be able to do my schoolwork, emailing it back and forth. And if things go well, I can stay all summer, returning for the start of the school year at Father Mercredi in September.

"But don't drink the water from the lake," she insists. "And don't eat the fish, either."

My grandfather reassures her. "That's one thing you *don't* have to worry about, Angela. We're not going to drink that water or anything that has any connection with it ... ever again."

I expect Frank to scoff at them, but he doesn't. "Best to play it safe," he says.

My grandfather leaves the next day, heading to Chip by air so that he can open up the cabin and prepare for my arrival.

Dad, Mom, and I are going to make the trip on the winter road. It's only mid-March, so it will be open for two more weeks. It will be cheaper than flying, and we'll be able to take many more things with us; supplies that my grandfather needs, things that are crazy expensive in Chip. Apparently that includes just about everything.

"Why don't they build a proper road that we can use at any time of year?" I ask.

Frank and Angela both roll their eyes skyward.

The sun is barely above the horizon when we head out of Fort McMurray on Highway 63, the truck bulging at the seams with everything except for the kitchen sink. Along with all of the obvious necessities, like my clothes and meds, we're taking the necessities of life that are way too expensive in Chip — food, water, and toilet paper! We're also taking a shovel, chains, emergency flares, blankets, candles, and flashlights, in case we break down and get stranded by bad weather, or in our case *good* weather. Warmth melts the ice. The possibility of us crashing through into the frigid marshes, rivers, or lakes is scary. I comment that life jackets aren't included in the emergency supplies. Frank says they wouldn't help since the cold would kill us pretty damn quick — but not to worry because they close the road long before thawing becomes a risk. My grandfather's voice pops into my head, asking who *they* are and how much *they* care about people heading up to Fort Chipewyan. I add a question of my own: Have *they* considered global warming?

Despite the early hour, there's a crazy amount of traffic on 63. It's not until after we pass all the mines that the traffic thins and the winter road starts. I'd expected something spectacular, like a clear sheet of ice, Disney-style, but in actual fact it doesn't look much different from a regular highway. It's a disappointment. There's a sign telling us that there are no services for 280 kilometres! Others warn us of steep hills and sharp bends.

So we're cruising along at eighty and wham, we go airborne, hitting our heads on the roof of the truck. Frank knows that slamming his foot on the brake will send us into a skid, so we slow down gradually, skittering along the rutted surface, our teeth rattling, until we pull up alongside a small car that's already off the road.

"He must have hit the same bad patch," Frank announces.

Angela and I tuck into chips and watch through the window as Frank attaches a tow rope to the car. We pull it back onto the road.

"He shouldn't be on this road with a car like that," Frank says as we drive away. "Even more stupid, he's alone."

But in short order, *we* are running into difficulty too. Even with four-wheel drive, the wheels spin on the next icy hill and we start to slip sideways, then backwards. It's a horrible feeling. We're totally out of control. You'd think I'd be used to that particular feeling, but apparently not. I hold my breath as we slide to the bottom and then take another run at it, all of us leaning forward and urging the truck onward, like it's a horse!

When we reach the summit, we're on top of the world. Frank stops, and we get out for a while to look at the view. It's really cold — the snow squeaks under our feet and the breath freezes in our nostrils — but it's so worth it. The Peace Athabasca Delta stretches out below us as far as the eye can see. It's covered in snow and ice, so I can't see the sedge meadows, the willows, the streams, and marshes that I know are there, but all the same, it's beautiful. The sun is low in the sky, barely visible behind thin cloud, but its halo glows eerily out of the haze. Angela slips her arm around my waist.

"Sometimes we can't see the sun, but it's always there," she says.

"There's been a lot of thick cloud for the last year or two," my father adds.

I know that my parents' words are about more than the weather. They're talking about life.

"Come on, let's go," Frank says, heading back to the truck. He puts it in the lowest gear, and we creep down the hill toward the first of the ice bridges beneath us.

Night falls quickly, and soon our high beams are shining brightly through the darkness. And then the heavens light up with neon green and purple: the Northern Lights. Frank stops the truck again and turns off the headlights. It's as if the sky is a stage with giant curtains hanging down from heaven. They float like flimsy fabric in a light breeze, rolling open and then rolling closed again. We get out of the truck and lie on the snow, staring upward, until we get too cold. Then we press on.

Finally, with the aurora borealis dancing around us, we read the sign: Fort Chipewyan, established in 1788. A warm glow shines from the windows of houses in town, but in no time we're back in darkness. Then it's just a few more miles to my grandfather's cabin on Sandy Bay. We turn off the road and bump down the track, ducking our heads as the truck passes under ice-encased spruce boughs. In the high beams, nature sparkles like diamonds. It's breathtaking. For an instant, before my father kills the headlights, I see the expanse of windswept frozen lake stretched out before us. It makes my heart soar.

In the years that I have been away, my grandfather has gone high-tech. There are outside lights illuminating the log cabin and a satellite dish on the roof! Frank has phoned ahead and my grandfather is at the door, waiting for us.

Before long, I am curled up in my old bed, snuggling under my favourite blanket and fitting my body around the lumps in the mattress. It feels good.

The next day, Frank is anxious to hit the ice road back to McMurray before it melts. He doesn't want to run the risk of getting stranded in Chip. For the longest while I'd been telling Mom that I'll be fine, and that she needs to start picking up the pieces of her life, just as Dad suggests, so I'm surprised to find myself saddened when she leaves. I hug her tight and feel a little teary-eyed. I hug Frank too. He rubs my back firmly and I rub his. He feels strong and dependable. With his closeness comes the realization that I have always been way too hard on him.

"I'm gonna miss you, Dad."

He grins from ear to ear.

Once my grandfather and I have waved them off, we go back inside. It's unbelievably quiet. We make tea and sit drinking it without talking. I gaze out the window at the wilderness, feeling the isolation and the solitude. I think, *what now?* This is where I had wanted to be, but now that I'm here — what happens next?

When I left Fort Chipewyan, all those years ago, it took me a while to adjust to living in McMurray with close to a hundred thousand people. At first, everything had been very confusing and very noisy.

Now I have to make the adjustment in reverse. The silence is crazy. It allows me to hear the fear inside. It gives me time to worry that the cancer will come back. If I keep really busy and preoccupied, I can keep that thought at bay, but with an idle mind, the idea rises up like a monster.

Coming here wasn't a good idea.

CHAPTER FORTY

White Chest starts the migration first. He flies west toward his mate's territory, but he will not meet up with Three Talons this early in the flight. He is merely travelling his established route, one that takes him toward the chain of mountains on the western seaboard. His wings beat at a steady pace until the foothills are in sight. Then the air changes, lifting him higher in the sky and carrying him northward.

After Leon hung up on me, I'd been mortified that I might have lost him as a friend. He had lifted me out of my pain and had kept me going so many times, but I'd been a real jerk and hurt him. I felt like total crap about it. I was really relieved when he answered my text and accepted my apology. And now we're cool.

Since arriving in Chip, I've been bored stiff, so I've been texting him a lot. I've been messaging Gemma nonstop too, but she's getting really slow at replying.

Unlike me and Leon, who are both stranded like a couple of beached whales, Gemma's got a life to live. I figure I'd better stop pestering her so much.

With nothing better to do, I'm spending time online, finding out more about the oil sands industry and realizing that it's not just *my* family that is split down the middle. People either hate it or love it. There's not really any middle ground! There are so many online articles, blogs, and opinions that it's hard to tell what the truth is versus what's propaganda, what's cover-up and what's venom from crazy people.

Then I get an email from the intern who asked all those questions when I was back in the hospital. She wonders if my grandfather and I would be interested in working on a community-based research project being organized by the University of Manitoba. If so, she'll arrange for one of the elders right here in Chip to drop by and tell us about it.

A few days later, Joe arrives. My grandfather knows him. They go way back. Joe explains the study to us. "If chemicals are leaking into the river, those same chemicals will build up in the bodies of the fish, as well as other animals and plants too. The university is collecting data on *everything* … to see what's safe to eat."

"Data?"

"It's a fancy word for information. It's simple. All you have to do is catch fish, bag them, and freeze them for the scientists to collect. They'll take them to the university and test them for chemicals that are connected to the oil industry, chemicals that are toxic to humans, things like mercury, arsenic, cadmium, selenium —"

My grandfather's face lights up in understanding. "If the fish are full of chemicals, it will mean that those same chemicals are in the river!"

"Exactly! If the fish *up*stream of the industry are healthy, but the ones *down*stream are so toxic that they almost glow in the dark, then it's a good indicator that the industry is contaminating the river. The government already has figures for how much of those chemicals it's safe to eat, so anything in the fish, or the moose, or the plants that's higher than those limits … well, we shouldn't be eating it, right?"

My grandfather explodes in a very rare moment of excitement. "*CSI: Fort Chip* has come!"

I can't help but laugh.

"Make that *CSI: Wood Buffalo*," Joe says. "We're collecting data from all over the region. But you can collect fish from right here, just a mile or two down the lake, close to the delta. I'll give you the kit."

He produces a box that looks as if it should hold fishing tackle. Inside there are Ziploc bags, a couple of Sharpies, and disposable gloves. He takes us through the process of bagging, labelling, and recording information. "There's just a couple more important things to remember," he says.

"It's getting complicated," my grandfather says, his enthusiasm waning.

"Not really," Joe says. "You just have to make sure there's no open fuel cans around when you're fishing. And make sure that you don't spill any gas when you fill the tank."

"Why?" I ask.

"Gas contains the same petro-chemicals the scientists are testing for, so if you contaminate the samples, you'll get a false positive. And wear these disposable gloves when you handle the fish for the same reason, in case you have anything on your hands. Remember — one pair of gloves for each fish. Don't be tempted to use the same pair to handle several fish. That's how samples get cross-contaminated."

My grandfather is looking a little overwhelmed.

"You'll get the hang of it," Joe says. "And then all you have to do is drop the baggies off at the freezer in town. You'll be a couple of research scientists in no time."

After Joe leaves, my grandfather has an idea. "We can photograph the fish too. That new phone of yours takes really good pictures. We can show that the fish are smaller than they were back in the old days. And that there are less of them — just like I told you."

"That's a problem," I say, hating to discourage him. "We've got nothing to compare our photographs with.

We don't have pictures of fish from twenty years ago, or pictures of fish that weren't born because their parents were swimming in poison."

He deflates a little, so I make a suggestion. "How about if we do our own research too? The university only needs us to collect the fish and bag them, but there's no reason why we can't photograph them as well, or collect our own data! We can weigh them and measure them. We can even see how many we catch in a certain period of time. That way, a couple of years down the road, we might be able to show that the fish are getting even smaller or scarcer."

"What are we waiting for?" my grandfather says, bounding to his feet like a teenager. "Let's go!"

"It's cold out there!" I protest. But my grandfather is off like a shot to gas up the snowmobile and find all the things we'll need. I dig a new note pad out of my school supplies and optimistically draw lines on the first page, heading columns with *Date*, *Fish type*, *Length*, *Weight*. My grandfather finds a spring scale, and I add the ruler and pencil from my math kit to the growing stack of things.

"Are you ready, Doctor Hawk?" my grandfather asks, obviously excited at the prospect of us being research scientists.

"Yes, I am, Professor," I reply.

CHAPTER FORTY-ONE

Three Talons' route is a little shorter than that of White Chest, but she too keeps to the eastern slopes of the great Rocky Mountains, using their lift to ease her flight. The expanse of land and sky under the birds' wings is so vast that White Chest and Three Talons will not see each other as they cover the three thousand miles toward the place in Northern Alberta where countless generations of their kind have mated and raised their offspring. For both birds it will be a long and exhausting journey, one they embark on without choice. It's in their wings.

Bundled up in snowmobile suits and balaclavas, we head out onto the lake, me sitting on the back seat of the snowmobile, the auger and fishing gear rattling along behind us in the sled. The flatness of the icy landscape is interrupted only by a few islands poking above the frozen lake, and the whiteness is broken only by the spruce trees that cling to their steep slopes.

My grandfather kills the engine but remains seated for a while. I figure that he's waiting for a spurt of energy to climb off and drill a hole in the ice. Suddenly I catch sight of something big and bulky at the top of a jack pine. It's at least six feet across and two or three feet deep.

"What's that, Professor?" I ask, pointing skyward.

"An old fish hawk nest," my grandfather replies. "They build them really strong."

"It looks sad," I say. "Like a house that's not lived in anymore, like it's waiting for the family to come back."

"They might," my grandfather says. "Fish hawks return to the same spot year after year. They find the same tree and fix up the old nest, rather than start from scratch. That way the nest gets bigger and stronger every year. If the original pair doesn't return, then it generally means they've died. But a good nesting site is like prime real estate. Another pair often takes it over and renovates!"

I can't help but think how thrilling it would be if a pair of osprey show up for the summer. It might even give me an in with Chrissie. Genius!

Aargh! Why do I keep doing this to myself?

Eventually my grandfather starts to climb off the snowmobile. I wriggle back, giving him room to swing his leg over, and then I take his spot and watch him drag the auger out of the sled. "Darn thing gets heavier each time I use it," he complains.

I'd help him if I had the energy, but I don't. He pushes the spiked tip into the ice, heaves the machine upright, and then fiddles with the engine, pushing the button to prime it, and setting the choke. Finally, he yanks on the cord. On the third try, the engine springs to life with a roar, vibrating and skittering on the surface of the ice. It sputters while he cuts the choke, searching for the sweet spot for the gas, and then he squeezes the trigger.

The auger spins so fast, it's a blur. It digs in quickly, spitting up shaved ice that would be perfect to make snow cones. In a few seconds, water is gushing onto the frozen surface of the lake. With the engine idling, my grandfather drags the auger ten paces across the frozen lake and bores another hole.

"That beats the old way," he says, diligently checking for oil and gas leaks as he takes the machine back to the sled. He hands me a lure. "I don't use live bait these days. I bought these beauties. The hooks are weighted so they sink to the bottom. That's where the fish are at this time of year, where it's warmer."

I find it vaguely amusing that the bottom of this icy lake could be anything close to warm.

He passes me the rod and then sits cross-legged on the ice and starts to lower his line into the hole.

"Wait!" I yell, reaching into my pocket for my iPhone. "We need to do this scientifically. "How long are we gonna do this for?"

"An hour?" my grandfather suggests.

"You've got to be kidding! It's minus twenty! How about half an hour?" I don't give my grandfather time to disagree. I set the timer. "Three, two, one. Go!"

Simultaneously, we toss our lines in the holes. As soon as I feel mine reach the bottom, I start the rhythmic up-and-down jiggle that I learned as a kid, trying to convince a *big* fish down below that a tasty *little* fish is swimming by.

We don't talk. It's crazy quiet. So quiet that I hear my pulse throbbing in my ears. I let the fishing line rise and fall to its rhythm. I watch my grandfather, hunched over the hole in the ice. I feel a surge of love rise inside me.

There's a gentle tug on my line.

I pull out the thrashing fish, sliding it over the ice a ways so it doesn't flip itself back into the hole. I almost grab the slippery body to pry the hook from its mouth but then realize I have my snowmobile gloves on. *Crap! Disposable gloves are such a pain.*

"Are you going to weigh and measure it now?" my grandfather asks.

"Nope. We've got to do this scientifically. We'll fish for the whole thirty minutes, then we'll take the measurements and record all of the information."

The walleye gasps out its life, and I drop the line back into the hole. It isn't until the fish stops thrashing that I realize it has two tails. I'm fascinated and repulsed at the same time.

"First catch of the day, and it's deformed!" my grandfather says. "The scientists will love that one."

We settle back into silence.

My breath hits the frigid air in puffs of steam.

"When Rose was alive," my grandfather says, "and when Frank was young, I liked to come out here ice fishing. I'd always go home with fresh fish, and that pleased Rose. But I stayed out longer than I needed to. It was peaceful. I liked breathing the fresh air and listening to my own thoughts. Then Rose died. After that I didn't come out here much. I didn't like listening to my own thoughts any more. Then you arrived, and I started ice fishing again, so you'd have good fresh fish — so you'd grow strong and healthy." He shakes his head and snorts. "Look where that got us."

"Do you really think it was the fish that gave me leukemia?"

He shrugs. "You ate a lot of it for the first eight years of your life. Everything we put in our mouths back then started off *here* in this water. But it's not like you eat something bad in the morning and you get cancer in the afternoon. It takes time."

My grandfather's voice is loud. I wonder if I should remind him we're supposed to keep it down so as not to frighten the fish, but I can't get a word in.

"There used to be a commercial fishery here, you know. It had been here for as long as I remember."

I'm shocked.

"It was good. It gave people an income. But it closed down."

"Why?"

"I guess word got out that the fish might be toxic. Nobody wants a deformed fish on their dinner plate."

"That's too bad." My words don't do justice to how I feel. Because I'm beginning to understand how much my people have lost. *My* people. I've never thought of the Chipewyan like that, or the Cree or Métis who live alongside us in Chip.

"The elders say that when we disturb nature, we have to ask if it will impact our children, and our children's children, right down through seven generations. If anything in nature is hurt by our actions, we shouldn't do it. But people these days — they don't see past their own noses. They think only about how they can profit in the short term."

My grandfather seems to have said all he wants to say, and we continue fishing in silence. I bury my face in my jacket. I look at the time again. Still fifteen minutes left. I'm not gonna make it! The mouth hole of my balaclava is already stiff with frozen breath. A fish bites! It's a distraction from the cold. Ten minutes left — my fingers are numb. Seven minutes left — I can't feel my toes. Six minutes — I catch a jackfish! *Crap!* My fingers are numb. I can't get the *stupid* disposable gloves on to take the *stupid* fish off the hook. Ice fishing is nuts! Two minutes left — *who's gonna know if I cheat?* One minute — *hold on just a few more seconds.*

Finally!

Five fish lie on the ice: two walleye, two jackfish, and a goldeye. One has two tails, one has a small lump on its side. The others look healthy to my eyes, but my grandfather says their colour isn't right. They're tinged with dull shades of pink and green.

None of them are as big as the ones in my grandfather's memory.

CHAPTER FORTY-TWO

As they fly, the birds gauge the air temperature, sensing that it is still too cold to make the final push into the north, so they don't rush their flight as they sometimes do. They take their time, fishing in rivers and lakes along the way. Arriving too early would be a deadly mistake.

Miss Barry from the school here in Chip drops by. She suggests that I come to class for an hour or two each day. It actually sounds like a good idea. I've had my fill of sitting around drinking tea, and I feel it's time to get back into the real world. But I'm worried about clothes. My hair has grown, so I don't feel quite so much like a cancer kid now. I'm not as puffy as I was. But my clothing insecurities won't go away — until I tell myself that Fort Chip is almost off the map — the Alberta map, at least. It's an afternoon drive from the Northwest Territories — we're talking midwinter, when there's a road. So how into the latest styles can these kids possibly be?

I'm the first one to get on the school bus because we live so far out of town. A few minutes later we stop at the Mikisew Cree Reserve. I'm shocked. Even the little kids are wearing Canada Goose jackets. Older ones bob to the beat that's obviously playing through their big expensive headsets. Others are preoccupied by cellphones. I don't make eye contact. I'm intimidated.

When we arrive at the school, it's nothing like I remember it. There's a big sign on the front thanking Shell for funding. I find the right classroom — a grade eight/nine split. There are eleven students. Twenty are registered, but eleven is considered a good turnout. They stare at me, which makes me think they don't want to be friends. But as soon as Miss Barry introduces me, recognition lights up some of their faces. It's cool to see how much we've changed since grade two. Nobody treats me like I'm weird. I feel accepted. But after just a couple of hours I'm exhausted, so I'm relieved that my grandfather arranged to pick me up before lunch.

I climb wearily into the truck, but as we pull out of the school entrance I find myself looking straight into the cemetery. Instantly I'm revived. I stare at the graves just beyond the chain-link fence with a fascination that I know is morbid, but it's like I'm a fish on the end of a line, getting reeled in against my will.

My grandfather turns the truck onto the street and accelerates toward home.

"Stop!" I yell, the command flying out of my mouth without permission.

He slams on the brakes and we both jerk forward.

"What is it?"

"Nothing," I say. "I want to go to the cemetery, that's all."

My grandfather slaps a hand against his chest, suggesting that I nearly gave him a heart attack for no good reason.

He reverses down the deserted road and parks next to the opening in the fence. I get out of the truck and walk down the avenue of big old spruces, between graves decorated with plastic flowers. I'm surprised that my grandfather follows me, because there are a lot of crosses in this cemetery, and I know what he thinks about religion. He says he had more than enough of it when he was in school.

I look up and scan the entire cemetery. It's huge. "There must be more dead people in Chip than live ones!" I blurt out.

My grandfather shrugs. "This community is the oldest settlement in Alberta. A lot of people have died since 1788."

We tread carefully between the tightly packed graves. A bunch of them are strewn with messages written on weathered paper and faded cards. Most of the graves have white picket fences around them, some falling over and grey with age, but others are new. I recognize the family names; their relatives are in my class. Some plots are small; one has a teddy bear leaning against the marker. I pause to subtract date of birth from date of death. It's upsetting. I need to move on. I look up and see that my grandfather is crying. I walk over to him and put my hand on his shoulder.

"Is Grandma Rose buried here?"

He nods, wiping his sleeve across his face.

"There's no cross," I say.

"The Catholics destroyed her life," he replies. "I wasn't going to let them watch over her for eternity."

We stand together in silence. I feel as though I should honour my grandmother in some way, but I don't know what to say.

"I wish I'd known her," is all I can come up with. He smiles and we walk on, slowing at many graves, telling me about the connection to his family, some distant, some close. The word "cancer" comes up a lot.

"When I buried Rose, all of this area right up to the fence was still grass. I can't believe how many people have died since then. We used to live long lives here. Of course, there was an accident now and again. I remember someone getting mauled by a bear. And a snowmobile went through the ice. A boat sank now and again. Sometimes a newborn would die, or a mother would die in childbirth, but overall, people here lived long, healthy lives. When you got too old to do all the work yourself, your family or neighbours would help. They'd share their catch or their hunt with you and cut your firewood. But now it seems the young ones are dying even before the old ones. Cancer doesn't care how old you are."

He sighs. It's a sound I am so familiar with.

CHAPTER FORTY-THREE

"There's a supply plane!" my grandfather shouts in response to the far-off drone of an engine. "Come on. Let's get moving."

This is my grandfather's ritual: watching the skies and driving to the store, hoping to be first in line to get our pick of the fresh produce. Not that I have an appetite for most of it. I generally turn up my nose, and my poor grandfather gets frustrated. Even the things I used to love, I just don't want them anymore. I do have cravings, though. Yesterday it was for moose stew, like I used to eat when I was a kid. But my grandfather says it's not safe to eat moose anymore. They eat water weed that grows in the lake, and of course they drink the water too, so he's not prepared to take the chance. Today my craving is for Rice Krispies, so I'm really hoping there will be some in this delivery. I want to eat them dry. My stomach won't tolerate the milk. Just the thought makes me want to puke. My grandfather says this is a good thing, because milk costs thirteen dollars a jug.

We get to the store too early and have to wait around for a while, so we walk up and down the aisles looking at the price of things on the shelves. It's outrageous.

"We're stuck between a rock and a hard place," my grandfather says. "We can't live off the land anymore — it's killing us. We can't earn a living trapping because there's no beaver and no muskrat — nothing left to trap! And who buys animal furs these days anyway? So what choice do we have other than to come here to buy food? But look at the prices! Ninety-two dollars for this turkey! It's no bigger than a duck. If it wasn't for Frank's wages, we couldn't afford any of this. Some people have no choice; they go back to eating moose and fish."

I pick up a Snickers. It's only two dollars.

"The cheapest food is the junk!" my grandfather says. "So people get overweight and get diabetes. Then the experts say that we're sick because of our lifestyle — and that we get cancer because we use tobacco."

Put like that, it's a big problem.

But it's my lucky day. We come away with two boxes of Rice Krispies, several cases of bottled water, and our staple diet: chicken nuggets, frozen french fries, and canned tuna. And of course, another carton of teabags, since my grandfather won't make the traditional teas. He doesn't trust anything that grows in or by the lake.

The nights are still cold, but the days grow longer and the sun gets warmer. The ice on the lake cracks and heaves, the noise echoing around the landscape like gunfire. Channels of ominously dark water seep between the cracks. I can't wait to launch the boat and go fishing the regular way. But it's taking forever for enough water to emerge from the ice.

We wait. My grandfather doesn't expect much from me. The only thing he asks is that I get outside every afternoon. It's no hardship, because in the sheltered spots the sun is so warm that I can sit out in a hoodie and jeans. I even have a special rock I can lean against to do schoolwork, a giant slab of pink granite that rises from the shoreline. I like to sit there, even after I've done my schoolwork, my back moulded into the smooth rock that seems custom-made for me.

I google *leukemia*, trying to see if there's a link to the oil industry. It seems Frank's right — young people all over the world get it. But then I find an article in the *Journal of Epidemiology* that points to a link between childhood leukemia and petroleum … when babies are exposed to petrochemicals in the womb. I read each complicated word over and over, trying to figure out exactly what the author is saying. Then I tell my grandfather.

"When was this written?" he asks.

"In 1994."

My grandfather's eyes well up. "More than twenty years ago, someone knew — someone told the world ..."

He drops his head into his hands and sobs.

I feel neutral, kind of numb. I keep searching.

I discover that for more than half a century it's been known that long-term exposure to benzene damages bone marrow and can possibly cause leukemia. I don't know what benzene is, so I sidetrack to find out. Benzene is a petrochemical, a natural constituent of crude oil. My heart leaps in my chest. I glance at my grandfather. He doesn't look as if he's up to the news yet, so I keep searching.

Finally, I find an article published in July 2014 that states, "Long-term exposure to benzene causes increased risk of AML."

AML is acute myeloid leukemia — my type of leukemia!

Long-term exposure? I guess eating oil-contaminated fish and drinking oil-contaminated water until I was eight would probably constitute long-term exposure. Not to mention the eight months when my body was putting itself together in my mother's womb.

Frank was wrong.

My leukemia has *everything* to do with the oil industry.

CHAPTER FORTY-FOUR

White Chest and Three Talons follow the Athabasca River through the oil sands, homing in on the nest they used last year. Nothing remains of the dead juvenile. The only evidence of the tragedy is the fishing net still entwined in the twigs and flapping in the breeze. The two birds circle the bulky platform and then fly on.

Soon, millions of migrating birds fill the sky, the collective memory of their ancestors drawing them to the place where two great rivers break into a hundred pieces and trickle through low-lying wetland. Ducks and geese settle on the shallow ponds, feeding and regaining their strength before making the final push to their breeding grounds in the Arctic. Some have been left behind, floundering in oil after mistaking close-by tailings ponds for this place of refuge.

White Chest and Three Talons don't stop. Their instincts drive them just a little farther, to the edge of the big lake. There, among the solitude and greenery of undisturbed forest, they find refuge. And for once, luck is on their side. They discover an old osprey nest at the top of a jack pine. They scan the sky for the owners, but no bird swoops from a great height screaming that this spot is already taken. All is quiet. All is still. So the pair settles on the platform of strong branches and twigs. White Chest watches with bright eyes as Three Talons uses her beak to fuss with the structure. As soon as she seems satisfied, the courtship ritual begins. White Chest swoops out across the water. It is just clear enough for him to see fish swimming close to the surface. He plunges his talons into the back of a goldeye and carries it skyward. Higher and higher he flies until he is little more than a dot in the heavens, and then he plunges toward Three Talons, pulling up close to her and hovering like a hummingbird. It is the most dramatic sky dance he has ever performed. Three Talons is impressed. She asks him to repeat the dance just one more time, and then she accepts his offering of fish. It is the answer that White Chest has been waiting for. The pair mate, and then they set to work remodelling the nest.

My grandfather fires up the little aluminum boat, and we head out for our first afternoon of data collection. We chug toward our designated spot, close to the delta. The water there is not crystal-clear like it is when you go the other way, northeast toward Saskatchewan, where emerald spruces are reflected in clear water, or where dazzlingly white sand dunes roll into the lake. Here, close to the delta, the water still carries sediment from its journey through the muskeg, but it has a beauty of its own, and I feel it's where I'm meant to be. What's more, it's close to the abandoned osprey nest that we saw in the winter. I'm really hoping that the owners will have returned.

After a while, we choose the perfect place to turn off the engine and cast our lines. It's in sight of the old nest! My grandfather hunches forward over his rod, but I lean back, soaking up the sun, waiting to feel the slightest tug of the line in my hand. It's so peaceful — I could easily nod off. The whir of beating wings brings me back from the brink of sleep. I jerk upright, rocking the boat. It's a fish hawk, flying right over me! It flaps skyward and settles on the old nest, gazing at us nonchalantly.

"Do you think it's the bird we saved?" I ask with more excitement than I've had for months.

"I doubt it," my grandfather says. "They live long lives, though, so it is possible."

He studies the bird through the binoculars that my parents gave *me* just before I came up here. He uses them more than I do, since his eyesight is not as sharp as it used to be.

"Hmm," he muses, focusing on the fish hawk. "It's a male. He has a large white cap, just like ours had. It made him look more like a bald eagle than a fish hawk, remember?"

My grandfather's words take me back to Chrissie suggesting that the bird on our driveway was a bald eagle. I wish I could go back in time and have that moment again. I wish I could go back and change my destiny. The fact that I can't makes me sad.

My grandfather passes me the binoculars. "Here! Take a look."

I fiddle with the lenses trying to get a clear image. Finally, I see him. He's magnificent, and I'm so excited. "There's another one!" I exclaim as a second bird flies into view. "The female, I think. She's bigger."

"We're too close to the nest," my grandfather murmurs, using a paddle to quietly ease the boat back. "We don't want to scare them off."

"Do you think anyone else knows they're nesting here?" I ask, following my grandfather's lead and whispering.

He shakes his head. "I reckon we're the only ones who know."

CHAPTER FORTY-FIVE

The thought of visiting the pair of fish hawks always brings a smile to our faces. When my grandfather picks me up from school, we're both impatient to get to the nesting site and see what the birds have been doing. It's my grandfather's day to drive the boat. He's doing it *so* slowly, like an old man, in my humble opinion. When *I* drive, I go fast enough to outrun the hordes of insects that are single-minded in their mission to bite or sting us, but he's going so slow that the horseflies have caught up. I'm having to swat like crazy. "If you open up the throttle a bit more, we might get there today!"

"We can't go any faster than this," my grandfather protests. "The deep water passage isn't so deep anymore. I have to go slow in case the boat bottoms out."

Knowing the reason for our slow progress allows me to relax. I spray my neck with DEET and wait it out, taking in the landscape as if I'm a tourist seeing it for the very first time. In a way, I am. Being confined by hospital walls, cut off from fresh air and everything green, has made me very enthusiastic about the wilderness. Just like a tourist, I keep taking photos on my iPhone.

A coyote rips into a dead fish that has washed up on shore. When he hears the boat getting closer, his hackles go up and he growls at us, but he stands his ground and poses for a photograph as we putter past.

"He doesn't look good," my grandfather comments. "He's thin, and his coat is sparse."

As soon as we pass, the coyote returns to feasting.

"Why has the water level in the lake dropped?" I ask.

"There's a dam up in the mountains," my grandfather explains, "so we don't get much water from the Peace River anymore."

"I thought it was the Athabasca that fed this lake."

"The Athabasca comes up from the south, but the Peace comes down the other way. They both pass through the delta and feed this lake. Years ago this whole area would flood now and again. The water would pour over the riverbanks and fill up all of the ponds and lakes and marshes around here. We'd go all over by canoe — paddle to the best cranberry patches, trap muskrat and beaver. They were good eating and gave us warm furs. I haven't seen a muskrat for years. There used to be thousands of them."

"What happened to them?"

"After they built the dam, the wetlands dried up. Their homes vanished."

"Why did they build a dam?"

"To make electricity for the folks in British Columbia."

"But what about us? And the wildlife here?"

"We're dispensable."

I've heard this phrase before. It's really beginning to sink in.

"Then, to make matters worse," my grandfather continues, "the oil companies take water from the Athabasca River. Someone told me that they use more than three barrels of water to make one barrel of oil."

"No!" I say. "They recycle the water. That's what they said when we were planting the trees, remember?"

My grandfather scoffs. "They might recycle some, but they still use one heck of a lot of fresh water from the river."

"How come they can just take it? They don't own it, do they?"

My grandfather shakes his head.

"*We* need water! All of life needs water! If I know this, how come the oil companies don't know it?"

"They know it," my grandfather says.

"Well, what about the government, or whoever it is that's supposed to take care of the environment. How come *they* don't know it?"

"They know it," my grandfather says, his voice remarkably calm. "The government gives the oil companies their licences!"

A surge of outrage hits me. It's all so unfair. So wrong.

My grandfather doesn't seem angry, not the way I am. He navigates the boat carefully through the shallow channel that leads toward the nesting site. "They won't stop until we've gone the same way as the beaver and the muskrat," he says. "They won't stop until there's no water left for them to take."

"What happens then?"

"They'll leave their mess behind and move on. They'll go somewhere else, where there's still fresh clean water. And they'll start all over again. It's like I've always said: They don't care about us. They never have and they never will."

When we get close to the nesting site, we turn off the engine and drift. The nest is high in the tree-tops, but the dead branches make for good visibility.

"Well, look at that," my grandfather says, peering through the binoculars at the female flying over us with something trailing from her beak.

"What's she carrying? Is it a snake?" I ask.

"No, it's just reeds. But she's missing a claw! The back one!"

"Let me see." By the time I adjust the binoculars, the bird is long gone. Next time she comes out of the nest, though, I'm ready. My grandfather is right; the female has only three talons on her right foot.

As the days go by, we're able to get closer and closer to the nesting site without disturbing the birds. They've become used to us, like we're part of the landscape. We know that the female has laid her eggs because she stays on the nest while the male goes fishing alone, flying slowly over the shallows close to the bank, focusing his gaze just beneath the surface. He hardly ever misses, his talons nearly always snagging the back of a fish. When he flies away, shaking water from his plumage, he reminds me of a dog coming out of the lake. I can't help but smile.

It's my turn to look through the binoculars. I watch the male deliver a lake trout to Three Talons, then he perches next to her and waits for her to start eating. But she squawks and pushes the fish out of the nest. We watch it fall to the ground. It's the first time we've seen such behaviour.

"Why did she do that?" I ask. "Trout are one of her favourites, aren't they?"

"Yes, they are. There must be something wrong with that one."

"It could be loaded with chemicals," I suggest. "Maybe that's why she won't eat it. We should try to find it and bag it for our data."

"Good idea! But ease over there real slow. We don't want to scare her off the nest by getting too close."

I pick up the paddle and use it to gently guide the boat toward the shore. The white-chested male takes to the air again. He flies out over the lake, swooping low over our boat before heading skyward.

"He's fishing in the deeper water now," my grandfather observes.

Shielding my eyes from the glare, I stare up at the bird, now high in the bright blue sky. He hovers, then pins his wings to his sides and plummets downward. Part of me falls along with him, the air streaming past me. Close to the water, he swings his legs forward so that his talons are close to his beak, then he plunges in, feet first. The weight of his catch threatens to pull him under, but he refuses to let go of the meal. Flapping his wet wings, he's soon airborne. With the fish wriggling in his talons, he flies right over us! He's so low that if I were to stretch up, I'd be able to touch him. Instead I duck, and cold water runs down my neck.

"It *is* the one we saved!" I exclaim. "He's checking us out. He knows us too! Why else would he fly so low, right over us?"

"With that big fish in his talons, maybe he couldn't get any higher."

We've seen the bird fly much higher with even bigger fish, so I figure that my grandfather is kidding, although sometimes it's hard to tell.

I watch through the binoculars as White Chest drops the fish in the nest. Three Talons pokes at the offering. She eventually eats it, but without much enthusiasm.

My grandfather points his chin toward the base of the jack pine. I follow his gaze. The same scrawny coyote is devouring the trout that Three Talons rejected.

"There goes our data!" he says.

CHAPTER FORTY-SIX

Miss Barry has been super helpful getting my education back on track. Most teachers don't stay long in Chip. They quit and go back to where they came from, sometimes even before the year is out, but Miss Barry is different. She's been here four years already, and she doesn't even go away for the summer vacations! Thanks to her, I'm almost caught up with my schoolwork. She's been in touch with Mercredi High in McMurray, and together they've agreed to give me a whole credit for a paper on leukemia. It will be a piece of cake. I know everything. I just have to type it up.

They are also giving me a credit for the fish study that I'm still doing with my grandfather. And if I finish a few other outstanding assignments over the rest of the summer vacation, then I'll only be missing *one* credit to qualify for entrance into grade eleven. But without this one lousy credit, they'll hold me back in grade ten. Miss Barry's been doing some creative credit designing. She says I can do a presentation for the community on a topic of my choice. Anything! As long as it's vaguely related to what I've learned over the last two years. This is my only hope of moving on into grade eleven, so I say yes, despite the fact that I'm terrified of public speaking. Just the *thought* makes me break out in a sweat. I tell myself that I don't have to do it for a while yet, so I don't have to worry about it for ages. But I am worrying about it all the same.

The days are hot. The hordes of biting insects have gone. My grandfather and I have been visiting Three Talons and White Chest almost every day for over a month. The eggs should have hatched, but Three Talons is still sitting on the nest, and White Chest is still fishing.

My grandfather and I are fishing too, pressing on with our research. We sit in the boat, close to the tall jack pine where the osprey are nesting, and we cast our fishing lines. It's become my favourite place on the planet. Waiting silently, in the peace and solitude, I think over ideas for the upcoming presentation. It's been weighing on me like a ton of bricks.

All I know so far is that I want to use leukemia as an example to show that when one thing in the human body goes wrong, it throws other things out of balance, causing sickness and even death. I want to relate that to the environment, showing that *all things* are interconnected. I want to point toward the oil sands industry as being the culprit. I want to speak out, I really do, but most people in Chip earn their living from the oil industry. Do they want to be told that their jobs have destroyed the habitat for countless creatures? Or have polluted the river, starting a chain reaction that has thrown so many other things out of whack? Do they want to be told that the industry may have given me leukemia, or my grandmother bile-duct cancer? Do they want to be told that it's threatening their own health? I'm sure that they already know all this. How can they not? But they *need* jobs. It's that Catch-22 situation. But the overriding question in my mind is, *Will they boo me off the stage?* My stomach knots up at the thought of the confrontation.

The other problem is this: the venue for my presentation is the Syncrude Youth Centre. I'll get booed off the stage for sure.

White Chest flies overhead again, sprinkling me with cold water. My eyes follow him back to the nest. I focus the binoculars, hoping to catch my first sight of a chick. Suddenly, Three Talons pushes something toward the rim of the nest. It looks like a chick, and I'm excited, but then it's over the side and gone.

"Oh my god," I exclaim. "Did you see that?"

My grandfather sighs. "That's too bad."

"What d'you mean? What just happened? Did she just kill her chick?"

"It must have been dead. But she might still have a live one up there. They usually lay two or three eggs."

But as we watch, Three Talons repeats the process. A second chick tumbles to the ground. And then a third.

All of a sudden, it's like I'm being turned inside out. I'm sobbing so hard that I can't get enough breath.

My grandfather tries to make light of things. "Keep this up and we'll have to bail out the boat," he says.

But I'm out of control.

Vaguely familiar images flicker into my mind: dead osprey chicks; eggs with no embryos inside; eggs with shells as fragile as tissue paper. Along with the images comes the smell of rotting fish. I lean over the side of the boat and heave.

My grandfather puts his arm on my shoulder. "You know that this is about more than the birds, don't you."

I don't know what he means. I'm struggling to catch my breath.

"Breathe, Hawk," he says, "like this." He takes big deep breaths, and soon I fall into rhythm with him, releasing my fingers from his arm. We sit in silence for a while. I look back toward the nest. Three Talons and White Chest are gone. I bet they won't return.

After a while, my grandfather speaks tentatively. "There's something we really need to do."

"I know," I say, paddling the boat toward the tall jack pine.

"Stay in the boat," my grandfather says, trying to climb out. "I'll do it."

"No!" I protest. "I want to."

He solemnly hands me three Ziploc bags.

The baby birds aren't difficult to spot. They lie sprawled on the ground at the base of the tree. They are almost naked, their talons too big for their scrawny, fragile bodies, their massive eyes hidden under closed lids.

I gently lift each chick and place it in a bag, thanking the small creature for offering its body for research and praying that its short life will count for something.

CHAPTER FORTY-SEVEN

Gemma is coming to visit! I can't believe it. We drive to the airport just outside of town and watch the Cessna Caravan land. It's the regular scheduled flight that holds nine people. When she climbs down the steps, I can barely contain my excitement. I rush across the few feet of tarmac to meet her. She hugs me tight and then stands back, holding me at arm's length.

"Look at you!" she exclaims. "I can't believe it. You look *so* good."

"Back at ya," I reply. "Do you have luggage?"

"Yeah. They're gonna need a forklift to get it off. Your mom sent a few things."

"It won't take them long," my grandfather says. "How was the flight?"

"Great! We flew over the oil sands. Wow! That's some messed-up land — and it goes on forever. The size of it shocked me."

"And you were flying at around nine thousand feet," my grandfather says. "Imagine what it's like at ground level."

"We went right over Suncor. White smoke was drifting from the chimneys and billowing over the tailings ponds and the river — it made the whole place look like a giant water park on a cloudy day."

"Looks can be deceiving," my grandfather says.

"I was horrified at how close the tailings ponds are to the river. Shit! Oops, sorry."

My grandfather laughs. "That's okay. It's a good word to use when it comes to describing the oil sands."

"I just don't get it," she confides. "What were they thinking putting those ponds right on the river like that? It looks like an accident waiting to happen. And then what?"

Here we go again — my grandfather and my friend are best buddies. Unless I do something, I'm going to be on the outside for the whole five days of Gemma's visit. I jump in. "If the ponds leak, then the river brings the crap right down here to us on Lake Athabasca. And that's not the worst of it. The Slave River leaves the lake and joins the Mackenzie."

"*Oh my god!*" Gemma exclaims. "Next stop, the Arctic!"

This thought silences us all for a good minute.

"One thing," Gemma says, "when you get past the mining area, and you're back over the forest, what's with all the criss-cross lines? It's like a giant sheet of graph paper — like they've put in roads for housing or something?"

"You mean the seismic lines? They are part of the *in situ* mining."

Gemma frowns.

"It's how they get to the bitumen that's low-down," my grandfather explains. "It's not as hard on the eyes as surface mining, eh? The forest stays in place … mostly. Surface mining gets everyone's attention because it looks so bad, but it only makes up about twenty percent of the total mining here. The rest is *in situ*."

How come my grandfather knows these things, and I don't! I'm glad that Gemma continues to question him so that I don't have to show my ignorance.

"How does it work?"

"They put pipes deep underground and then force steam and chemicals down to melt the tar right off the sand. Then it's pumped to the surface and to a processing plant. Less damage is done to the earth's surface —"

I interrupt, trying to show that I have a brain in my head. "That must use a lot of energy, heating the steam and all."

My grandfather nods. "There's another problem too, one that people don't seem to care about. The seismic lines break the old growth forest into small chunks. It's hard for the animals, especially the woodland caribou."

"They're on the brink of extinction!" Gemma exclaims. "Is that why?"

"Yes. They've lost their secluded habitat and their migration paths. Then the wolves are the final straw — they lope along the seismic lines for a quick meal."

"Fast food for wolves," I joke. I know this is far from funny, so I'm not surprised when Gemma scowls at me and smacks my arm. But I'm on a roll and can't stop myself. "One McCaribou Happy Meal coming up!"

My grandfather doesn't even hear me. He's on a roll too. "The government says the caribou are endangered because the wolves are eating too many of them! It's true. But instead of trying to solve the real problem, they go shooting the wolves from helicopters!"

"No way!" Gemma says, aghast. "That's wrong. The wolves aren't to blame."

I'm hearing this for the first time … I think. But there's a familiarity to it that makes me wonder if my grandfather told me about it before and I forgot. It's confusing and not the first time this kind of thing has happened. I sometimes wonder where I went when I was in the coma.

Gemma wasn't kidding about her bag. It's huge. Even my wiry grandfather struggles to lift it into the back of the pickup. She apologizes. "Angela told me that everything up here is expensive, so she sent me with a frozen chicken, some steaks, ten pounds of potatoes, and a few other things!"

My mouth waters at the thought!

We give Gemma the guided tour of Chip. It takes five minutes. It's the first time she's been to a First Nations community, and she's surprised by the town's paved roads and the sidewalks, the street lights, and the new construction. "Even the old houses are being done up," she comments, looking at new siding going up on one house and new windows going into another.

"What did you expect?" I ask. "Wigwams and teepees, or broken-down trailers?"

"Neither, but I expected it to be a bit more rundown, you know. We hear about northern communities, that everything is so …"

"Shitty?" I suggest.

"And the people are so …"

"Drunk?" I say.

"C'mon! I didn't mean that … well, not exactly."

"It's the oil money," my grandfather says. "You can tell who works in the industry. They are the ones with new trucks in the driveway. And the fancier houses."

"There's lots of new trucks," she observes. "And lots of nice houses."

We stop at the Northern, not because we want to buy anything but just so Gemma can see the prices. She takes a photo of a sad wedge of watermelon priced at fifteen dollars and another of four overripe tomatoes at eleven, just so people in McMurray will believe her.

Then we head up to the Archie Simpson Arena. It's almost deserted. Two young kids shoot pucks on the state-of-the-art ice rink. No toddlers are in the children's play area. The Syncrude Youth Centre is empty. And not a single weightlifter works out at the gym. We show Gemma the adjacent site where work is underway for the indoor water-park that will have a twenty-five-metre pool, complete with waterslide, hot tub, and sauna.

"How many people live here?" she asks.

"Just over a thousand," I reply.

"*Shut up!* I hate to say this, but don't you think they're trying to buy your silence?"

My grandfather nods. "What's more, they're going to link the new water park to the existing arena to make one enormous complex. The whole community could live here! If they add a place to eat, we need never go outside, ever again!" He's joking, but sadness sweeps over him. "The old life is over."

CHAPTER FORTY-EIGHT

We're cooking dinner the traditional way. We get a fire going in the pit on the beach and wait for what seems an eternity until the wood burns down to glowing embers. The potatoes go in, wrapped in foil — my grandfather's one concession to living in the twenty-first century. An hour later the steak goes on. It sizzles and smells so good. We don't have to wait long. My grandfather gets it perfect! Gemma says it's the most delicious meal she's ever eaten, and I have to agree. With our bellies stuffed, we sit around the fire watching the sparks disappear into the twilight of the night sky. My grandfather goes to bed, but Gemma and I lie on our backs gazing up at the stars. More and more of them come out until there are more stars than bare sky. They won't twinkle for long — it's midnight, and soon they'll fade into the light of dawn. For once Gemma is silent. I hear the waves lapping gently against the shore. After a while I wonder if she's gone to sleep, but she hasn't. She's still staring at the stars, mesmerized.

"It's really nice here," she finally says.

"I know! We can take the boat out tomorrow, if you want."

"Cool!"

I don't want to go toward the delta. I don't want to be reminded of the osprey, so we head up the lake, toward Saskatchewan, stopping at the sand dunes to eat lunch.

"Can we go swimming?" Gemma asks, tempted by the clear blue water.

"Sure," my grandfather replies. "Come back in a year or two when the water park is finished!"

It's Gemma's last night. The five days have flown by, and I'm sad that she'll soon be leaving. We've talked about a lot of things, including me possibly doing the presentation to earn a credit, and the cold feet that I have about it.

"Hawk! You've got to do it," she shrieks. "Get over yourself. Sure, it's a challenge, but nothing compared to the challenges you've been through recently. And it'll look good on your resumé."

What's with all the significance of resumés? I'll be happy if my resumé says nothing more than "survived leukemia."

"Do it!" she orders. "Besides, if you don't, I'll be in grade eleven and you'll only be in ten. You know how bad that's gonna make you feel? And then I'll go off to university, and you'll be left behind."

The conversation progresses naturally to careers. She tells me about her plans to be a sports physiotherapist."

"Wow. That sounds custom-made for you. I wish I knew what I was going to do in the future. Or if I have a future! I'm in remission, but how long will that last?"

"I can't imagine how hard that must be," she says, "but all the same, you have to plan for a future … at least, that's what I think."

"I'm trying to," I say. "It's just that I don't know how — or where — or what to do. How did you figure you wanted to be a sports physiotherapist?"

"We had a career fair at Mercredi. People came to talk about different careers. As soon as I heard about sports physiotherapy, I knew it was for me!"

"We had a career day too," I tell her. "The oil companies came. No one else. They said we could drive 797s, like Frank. Most of us think that would be the coolest job ever — driving the biggest truck in the world."

"Boys and their trucks," Gemma says judgmentally. "Didn't they suggest anything else?"

"Sure. Pipe fitting, carpentry, electrical — any of the trades that the industry needs. You can get trained at Keyano College in McMurray, so they make it easy for us."

"What about being a chemical engineer, or an environmental scientist working on reclamation?"

I scoff. "I doubt they think we're smart enough for university. Anyway, we don't have a science lab."

"What?" Gemma shrieks.

"Crazy, eh? It's the only school here! The oil companies pay for so much in town, and they've put money into the school, but no science lab."

"Why not?"

"My grandfather says they don't want us learning science in case we figure out what's really happening in the oil sands and start making trouble."

"*Oh my god*, Hawk! You gotta do that presentation! You gotta get people caring *more* about their land and water and *less* about a big paycheque."

"It's not that simple," I say. "People here need jobs, they need incomes."

"Surely they can get other jobs, even if they pay less."

"That's the problem. There's no other work! And thanks to the industry, we can't live off the land the way we did in the old days." *I'm using the word "we." What's happened to me?*

"We can sit on our butts and do nothing," I continue, "and prove to the outside world that we're lazy and good-for-nothing, just like they've always said.

Or we can work in the industry. There aren't many other choices."

"I didn't realize," she says. "It's more complicated than I thought."

She picks up a pamphlet and hands it to me. "Have you seen this?"

"What is it?"

"*Historical Highlights of Fort Chipewyan.* I got it at the museum this morning. It says there was an oil spill here in 1981."

"No way!"

She points to the place on the time line. "The Suncor Oil spill in Fort McMurray affected the water and fish as far as Fort Chipewyan."

"When?" my grandfather asks, appearing out of thin air as he often does.

"In 1981."

He shakes his head. "Unbelievable. Our food and water was contaminated by an oil spill in 1981, and I never knew! Everything in the lake — everything that depends on the lake for food and water — *everything* would have been poisoned. Including Rose."

I'm already online, trying to find something that supports this one sentence, this one event so many years ago that may have changed our lives. The Internet is silent.

But then I find a stunning piece of information on Wikipedia. "In 1997, Suncor admitted that their tailing ponds had been leaking 1600 cubic metres of toxic water into the river a day. This water contains naphthenic acid, trace metals such as mercury, and other pollutants."

"How much is 1600 cubic metres?" I ask.

Gemma googles conversions. "One point six million litres."

"*Holy shit!*" I say. "That's eight hundred *thousand* big bottles of Coke … a day!"

Gemma comes up with another way to visualize it. "Or thirty-six backyard swimming pools! A day!"

"How many days was it leaking for?"

I reread the article. "It doesn't say."

She's outraged. "How could it not say? That's important information, isn't it? I mean we could be talking two days, or two hundred days, or even two thousand."

Then the significance of the date hits me like a Mack truck. It was 1997! A couple of years later, as I grew in my mother's womb, as the marrow in the centre of my bones was created, I was fed a diet of heavy metals and petrochemicals. I remember telling Chrissie that the baby osprey were the first to show the effects of toxicity. My mother, like the female osprey, was also at the top of the aquatic food chain!

CHAPTER FORTY-NINE

Gemma suggests I make a PowerPoint presentation on my iPad so that when I give the talk — if I give the talk — I won't be tied down to paper notes. She says I can import photographs from my phone and download others from the Internet, and arrange them in a slide show to help tell my story. Apparently, I'll be able to hook my iPad up to the projector at the Syncrude Youth Centre and show it on the screen, yet still see my notes on the iPad! Cool.

"Promise me you'll do it," she says.

Gemma doesn't make it perfectly clear what "it" means — probably the presentation in front of the community. But "it" might mean making the presentation on my iPad.

"I promise," I tell her, opting for the latter.

It's done, except for deciding on the title. *Hawk's Battle*, maybe, or *A Battle of the Hawks*. But whatever the title ends up being, the presentation is gonna be about White Chest and his struggle to raise a family and ensure the survival of his species, related to my own struggle against leukemia and the survival of my people here in Chip. There are so many similarities between me and White Chest. We're both at the top of the food chain, both eating fish from the same river, both fighting for survival. We even share the same name. It's eerily weird that my grandfather named me Hawk. Of course, *he* wouldn't use the words *weird* or *eerie*. He'd say he was guided by the ancestors and that the Spirit of the Hawk watches over me. Sometimes I think he might be right.

I really enjoyed putting the presentation together, and when I ran through it out loud in my own room, I figured it was half decent. But every time I envision myself actually presenting it … in front of *people*, I seriously feel like throwing up.

I asked Miss Barry if *she* could present it for me. She wouldn't hear of it. She says it's my story, and I'm the one who has to tell it. But my stomach is tied up in knots all the time. I know it's crazy, but, honestly, I'd rather spend a whole extra year in high school than give one stupid presentation. So I make the decision. I'm not doing it.

I'm on the beach, sprawled out on the sand under the late summer sun, relaxing. It feels great. A loud snort makes me sit bolt upright, memories of the cancer bull coming to me in a scary rush. Not twenty feet away, a *caribou* bull steps out of the bush onto the shoreline. He's big! I'm almost scared to breathe, terrified that he'll charge me. But his eyes are soft, and there's nothing threatening about the way he stands. His coat is rich and tawny, and white hair flows under his neck like an upside-down mane. From the belly up, he's majestic, his head topped with massive antlers, just like you see on the Canadian quarter, but from the belly *down* his over-sized hooves and crazy long legs give him a funny, cartoonish look. And his tail! Well, it looks as if it belongs on a rabbit! He curls back his upper lip, searching for the scent of a female. I haven't seen caribou all summer long. I suspect that there are none around here. I sense his loneliness. I relate to it.

I remember the reclamation project at Energyse: *When all the oil is dug from the sand, trees will be replanted and forest will again cover the landscape, and the animals and birds will return.* But will the woodland caribou return? Will there be any left to return? And what will they eat? They feed on the lichens that grow in the old growth forest. It takes 150 years for trees to become old and eighty years for lichen to grow on them.

He turns, and with his gawky gait, ambles into the trees. He grunts. To my ears it sounds like a sigh of defeat. His species doesn't have that kind of time.

I sigh and reconsider my decision about giving the talk. Again.

There's a faint smell of smoke in the air. It's not the smell that sometimes floats up from the oil sands industry; it's a forest fire burning in the west. Miss Barry says that there are more wildfires this year than ever before because of global warming and drought. The wind is bringing it our way. It's scary. If the smoke is coming our way, the flames won't be far behind. In Edmonton or Calgary or even Fort McMurray we'd be evacuated, but I'm not expecting anyone to airlift us out of here. My grandfather, with his quiet way of dealing with all upheaval, tells me not to worry, because if the fire swoops down on Fort Chip, we have plenty of water to douse the flames, and worst-case scenario, we abandon ship in reverse — we load as much as we can into boats and get out on the lake. We might lose everything that's left on land, but at least we'll be safe. All the same, he's watching the skies like a hawk, and I can tell he's making plans.

The wind shifts and we get a reprieve.

Summer is fading. I'm sitting cross-legged on the beach, reading the last novel for my English course. The story has me hooked. It's about the Holocaust.

It's unbelievably sad, and it makes me wonder why there are no books on the curriculum about *my* people and *our* holocaust. Is it as my grandfather says … we aren't important? I can't totally accept it. I hope it's as Gemma suggested … that people just don't know. Someone needs to tell them. *Oh, crap!* Maybe that someone is me.

I can see my grandfather in the distance, heading back across the lake toward the shore, and my heart warms at the sight of him. The beach is bigger now than it used to be, a longer expanse of gritty sand leading to the water's edge. It looks inviting, but I know it's not a good thing. The level in the lake is falling. The oil companies are taking more and more water from the Athabasca River, dumping more and more contaminated water into more and more tailings ponds. They are making the ponds deeper and bigger, making them stronger and safer. But placed along the edge of the Athabasca as they are and lined with nothing more than hard-packed clay, it seems to be a recipe for disaster. And nobody seems to have a long-term plan. How can toxic tailings ever be disposed of safely? I wish someone would tell me.

In the old days, miners would take caged canaries into the tunnels underground. If the canaries dropped dead, it meant that the air was unsafe to breathe and the miners needed to get out in a hurry. Canaries were the early warning system. The muskrats that my grandfather used to trap … were they our early warning system? And the beavers? And my grandmother? The world didn't heed the warning, and now others are getting sick, people like me. And birds like White Chest's babies. Are we the new early warning system? If we are ignored, then what?

My grandfather reaches the shore, and as I help drag the boat up the beach, I remember that just a month or two back I was too weak to do this. I've come a long way. The honking of geese stops us both in our tracks, and we look up to watch them. They fly low over our heads in a ragged V formation, their beating wings whirring the air. I am thrilled to see them, but my grandfather is disappointed.

"Twelve," he counts. "When I was a boy there would be so many water birds at this time of year, the sky would be filled with them. Every year there are fewer. Take a good look, Hawk. Who knows what the future will bring."

CHAPTER FIFTY

It's crunch time. Not only am I doing the dreaded presentation, but there's now a crazy amount of hype. Miss Barry says that it's shaping up to be the main event of the summer. *Why would she tell me that when she knows how nervous I am?*

None of this buildup is a reflection on *me* and my transformation into a superstar. It's more a reflection of the fact that we don't have a movie theatre here in Chip, so entertainment is seriously lacking. Also, it's because Miss Barry has been working her butt off. She made posters and put them up all over town. When I stopped by the Northern for a Twix, I was shocked to see a life-sized photo of my face staring back at me. Same thing at the Syncrude Youth Centre. "HAWK'S-EYE VIEW," the caption reads. Then in smaller print: "Hawk shows us the parallels between his own battle with leukemia and the battle that rages in the natural world here in the Wood Buffalo Region."

Huh! That's why Miss Barry took a photo of me and asked for a one-liner on what I was going to talk about. She didn't mention the oil sands on the poster, though, even though she knows that's gonna be a big part of my presentation. Smart. Apparently my face also stares down at visitors to the museum, the post office, and the emergency clinic! You'd have to be blind *not* to know about me and my talk. Miss Barry even emailed the principal, but like most of the teachers, she's away for the summer. Word is that she'll be back in town the same day of my talk. I'm hoping she gets delayed.

Two hundred chairs already filled.

Standing room only.

Waiting to be introduced.

Seriously cold feet.

Seriously sweating palms.

Miss Barry is speaking, saying nice things about me, I think, but her voice is coming and going in distant waves.

Heart pounding.

Knees shaking.

Damn! There's a lot of people out there. I wonder how many of them have family working in the industry. All of them, I'm sure!

Damn it! I should have gone to the bathroom.

Be still. Be present. Breathe.

Palms still sweating.

"And now, let's give a warm welcome to Hawk."

I wouldn't call it a roar of applause, but there's some clapping for sure. And no booing. I walk to the podium, where my iPad is already hooked up to the projector and screen. My knees threaten to give way. Miss Barry smiles as she passes me the microphone, but my hands are shaking. I don't want everyone to see how nervous I am, so I whisper for her to put it on the stand instead.

I tap the first slide. It's a photo of White Chest, the best one from my collection. I turn my head to see if it projected onto the screen. It did. It's huge and crystal-clear. White Chest is standing on the rim of the nest, his enormous bright yellow eyes staring down at me. It's a stunning picture, even on my laptop, but on the big screen it's breathtaking. I'm almost hypnotized by the transparency of his eyes. Then I hear a question in my head that is so un-hawk-like that it almost makes me laugh. *What do you say, bro, we do this together?*

I smile, lift the microphone from the stand, and speak. I have a voice! It sounds amazingly strong, so strong that it surprises me.

"This is White Chest …" I begin.

A presence comes over me that's hard to describe. It's like flying! Like being on a flight path that has been mapped out especially for me! It's a strange new feeling, yet at the same time it's an old familiar one. I can't wrap my head around it, but I don't need to. I just need to accept it and go with the flow.

I feel empowered.

I speak from my heart, not even reading the notes on my iPad. Instead, my eyes move back and forth across the audience, taking it all in. I spot the principal. Her eyes are glued to me, and strangely, her presence doesn't make me feel like crapping my pants. I see my grandfather. He's hanging on my every word. I see some of my classmates, sitting together at the back. They're not having private conversations, as I would have expected them to. They are listening! In fact, throughout the entire audience people seem to be giving me their undivided attention. There's no heckling! The time races by. I'm enjoying myself, and I don't want it to end.

"Thanks for being such a fantastic audience," I say, wrapping up. "It's been great to share all this with you."

And I mean it!

Instead of hightailing it to the exit, people clap, and although there are a few sad faces, I feel love and support.

Then I'm mobbed, people patting my shoulders, shaking my hand, giving a hug or a high-five. My principal touches my arm. "Congratulations Hawk. That was powerful."

Powerful! Seriously?

My grandfather waits in the background until the crowd has thinned. "The hawk came through, eh? Just as he promised."

I nod.

"TED Talks next," he says.

I laugh, assuming he's kidding, but looking at his face it's hard to tell.

CHAPTER FIFTY-ONE

I stand on the beach, gazing out over the lake. It's the end of August, my last morning in Chip — time for me to move back to McMurray. There should be a chill in the air, but although a band of mist hangs over the glassy surface of the lake, the sky is bright blue, and I can tell it's gonna to be another glorious day. Briefly I contemplate the link between the oil sands industry and global warming, but then more urgent things distract me. I have less than an hour to commit everything around me to memory. I fear that the weight of urban life will steal this place from me, so I need to stockpile the details. I've taken a million photographs, but I need to breathe the air and take in the smells, hear the sounds and let it all sink in.

I have such mixed feelings. My grandfather is staying in Chip, determined to continue his research. It will be hard to say goodbye. I'll miss him. But on the other hand, I'm looking forward to seeing Mom and Dad again and to starting a new phase in my life, one that not long ago I figured I wouldn't have; a life in which I'm known as Hawk, not Adam, a life where my long hair will be tied in a ponytail, and where I'll make a difference. I feel hopeful, accepting, and strong. But I'm realistic too. I know that cancer has a way of ruining your plans. I know that this may be the last time I ever stand here.

So I'm sad. But I drink it in, sadness and all.

The lake is peaceful, as it often is in the early morning. There are no whitecaps in the distance, and no waves rolling up on shore, just the gentle lapping of sleepy water against cool sand. The bush drips with dew, so heavy that the leaves droop under the weight. A spider sits in the centre of a perfectly spun web that is strung across the trail, like a hammock slung between two trees. I know for sure it wasn't there yesterday. My mind is blown that such a small creature can spin such a smart trap in so little time. It's genius! But it's so fragile! It can be destroyed so easily, by the touch of a human hand.

I duck under the web and walk down the beach to the water — the water that has given life to my people since the beginning of time, but water that may now be killing us. Before I got leukemia, I didn't have any idea of what I wanted to do with my life, but now I know, and whether I live to be eighteen or eighty, I intend to make good use of every day. I won't let fear steal that away from me. I'm going to help protect our planet, and I'm going to start by speaking out for the creatures who are voiceless.

I pick up a smooth, round pebble and hurl it out to where the surface is smooth as glass. It skips and sinks. Ripples radiate out in small circles, growing bigger and bigger.

It strikes me that now is the time to start making ripples. I plan to make some big ones, so that after I am gone they will still remain.

That's good enough for me.

After the young man and the old man had visited for the last time and had taken away the dead chicks, White Chest wooed his mate once more. No human eyes saw his magnificent sky dance. Driven by the need for the species to survive, Three Talons laid one more egg, but it was already late in the season. The chick hatched, but it was a race against time.

The parents fished through the rapidly shortening days. Without siblings to share the catch, the single chick grew quickly.

But summer was fading fast.

And maturity takes time.

The young bird's soft down was replaced by adult feathers, but they did little to fend off the deepening cold of the approaching Alberta winter. She grasped the edge of the nest with her talons and flapped her young wings. The movement warmed her.

In the way of the osprey, Three Talons perched on an open branch a short distance away with a fish in her grasp. Over and over, she called to her offspring, encouraging her to fly.

But the young bird was not yet strong enough to make her first flight.

She needed more time.

Nature was kind. September was unusually warm. But then a cold rain fell, and all three birds shivered.

White Chest left first, his need to survive sending him south to where the warm sun gives life.

Three Talons spread her wings over the young bird, protecting her from the elements, as she did when she was a chick. By morning, the forest sparkled with a faint glimmer of ice. Three Talons had no choice. She too flew away from the nest, heading south.

The young osprey blinked her red eyes, watching her mother vanish into the distance. Then she launched herself into the air. On unsteady wings and on a wavering flight path, she followed.

AUTHOR'S NOTE

THE OSPREY (FISH HAWK)
These large fish-eating raptors are at the top of the aquatic food chain in many of the world's river systems. As such, they are sensitive to toxins that build up in the bodies of fish. Two interesting facts: they close their nostrils to keep out water during dives; they have barbed talons to hold the fish and align it, reducing drag while in flight!

WOODLAND CARIBOU and WOLVES
Caribou are the only member of the deer family in which both males and females grow antlers. The woodland caribou eat lichen that grows on old-growth trees. The oil sands industry has removed both their habitat and their food source. Since wolves also prey on caribou, provincial wolf culls are underway to help save the dwindling caribou population from extinction.

THE OIL SANDS

Originally called the Tar Sands, the Athabasca Oil Sands is the largest known reservoir of crude bitumen (tar) in the world. Each grain of sandy soil under the ancient boreal forest and wetland is coated with bitumen. Removing, separating, and processing this bitumen into synthetic crude oil uses large amounts of water and heat, causes devastation to the land, and generates toxic tailings.

FORT CHIPEWYAN

The Athabasca River flows through the oil sands to Fort Chipewyan on the shore of Lake Athabasca. For over a century, Cree, Chipewyan, and Métis trappers traded furs here: fourteen beaver pelts for one gun; one pelt for five pounds of gunpowder; two for one pound of tobacco. From here, Canada's great explorers and mapmakers charted territory that defined the North. Today, few residents live off the land and many work in the oil sands. From Fort Chipewyan, rivers flow north toward the Arctic.

ACKNOWLEDGEMENTS

I am grateful to the Ontario Arts Council for the Writers' Reserve Grant that helped me travel to the Athabasca Oil Sands and Fort Chipewyan to research this story.

I thank Feroze Mohammed for reading this manuscript countless times and for teaching me to strive for flawlessness.

I thank my daughter Joanna, for her excellent ideas, for travelling with me to Fort Chipewyan, for flying with me over the oil sands in a terrifyingly tiny plane, for taking photographs, and for never allowing me to settle for writing anything other than my very best. And I thank my daughter Kate, for holding the fort at home so that I could write and travel, for her incredible insight into story-writing and her vision for this book.

I thank Fort McKay residents Janice and Barbara, who started an uncanny chain of events at the Athabasca River that led me to Dr. John O'Connor. And I thank John O'Connor and Charlene for their enthusiastic response to my writing and for being a true inspiration. I'm sure their grandchildren, Quinn and Blair, will help make the world a better place.

I thank my new friends in Fort Chipewyan for supporting me in this project and helping me get the story right, especially Tatana Kejla (nurse practitioner); Kathy Inglis (palliative care nurse); Marjorie Glanfied (reverend of St. Paul's Anglican Church); Karen Maria (museum curator) and her wonderful mother, Gracie; and Bruce Inglis for fishing advice. Also the staff and students of Athabasca Delta Community School, Fort Chipewyan, especially teacher Tegan Vacheresse and her grade eight/nine students: Kierra Voyageur, Keisha Bourke, Emma Voyageur, Brianna Waquan, Dawson Mercredi, Alanis Courtoreille, Dominic Marten-Shott, Jeremy Maten, Keannah Cardinal, Kara Tourangeau, and Samuel McDonald.

I am also grateful to Charlotte Gobbens for her dedication to the osprey and her webcam footage; to Linda Hutchison, Darlene Campbell, and Betty Scuse for their prayers and support; to editors Allison Hirst and Allister Thompson, who took my work and made it better. And to my manuscript readers: Jane Warren, Matthew Mohammed, Dr. Amy Miller, Christine Perrault, Elizabeth Pasek, Jeni Barchard, Cathy Passafiume Wood, Noah Wood, Jennifer Greenham, Jenn Scuse, Gail Aziz, Josi Norton, Elizabeth Donaldson, Laura Shin, Amy Harris, and Wes Coultice.

MORE BY JENNIFER DANCE

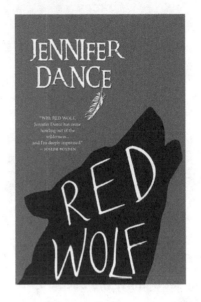

RED WOLF

MOONBEAM CHILDREN'S BOOK AWARDS 2014 — SILVER MEDAL
FOREST OF READING, SILVER BIRCH AWARDS — SHORTLISTED
MYRCA AWARD 2016 — SHORTLISTED

"WITH *RED WOLF*, JENNIFER DANCE HAS COME HOWLING OUT OF THE
WILDERNESS ... AND I'M DEEPLY IMPRESSED."
— JOSEPH BOYDEN, GILLER PRIZE–WINNING AUTHOR

**Life is changing for Canada's Anishnaabek Nation and for the wolf
packs that share their territory.**

In the late 1800s, both Native people and wolves are being forced
from the land. Starving and lonely, an orphaned timber wolf is
befriended by a boy named Red Wolf. But under the Indian Act, Red
Wolf is forced to attend a residential school far from the life he knows,
and the wolf is alone once more. Courage, love, and fate reunite the
pair, and they embark on a perilous journey home. But with winter
closing in, will Red Wolf and Crooked Ear survive? And if they do,
what will they find?

PAINT

The life story of a painted mustang set against the backdrop of America's Great Plains in the late 1800s.

It's the late 1800s. When a Lakota boy finds an orphaned mustang and brings her back to his family's camp, he names her Paint for her black-and-white markings. Boy and horse soon become inseparable, and learn to hunt buffalo, their fear of the massive beasts tempered by a growing trust in each other.

When the U.S. Cavalry attacks the camp, the pair is forced onto separate paths. Paint's fate becomes entwined with that of settlers, who bring irreversible change to the grassland. Bought and sold several times, Paint finally finds a home with English pioneers on the Canadian Prairie.

But with a great dust storm looming on the horizon, man and horse will need to work together if they hope to survive.

....

jenniferdanceauthor · @ JenniferDance1 · jenniferdance.ca